The Introvert Series (compiled into one fun book)
Jessica Terry

The Introvert Series Compilation

Jessica Terry

Published by Jessica Terry, 2023.

This is a work of fiction. Similarities to real people, places, or events are entirely coincidental.

THE INTROVERT SERIES COMPILATION

First edition. January 9, 2023.

ISBN: 979-8986432199

Written by Jessica Terry.

I so loved this series and thought it would be so cool to see them all packaged together. The response to these stories has been awesome and I'm thrilled my introvert Lola is loved so much. Thanks a million to everyone who has left a review or a kind word about her or her crazy friends. :)

An Introvert's Christmas

ONE

Sigh.

So this was the deal. It was two days before Christmas and I had just been dumped.

Bummer, but I wasn't that broken up about it. Orlando and I weren't really going anywhere, anyway. It wasn't like I was madly in love or anything. And when a man up and dumps you because you accidentally stepped on his PlayStation controller, you probably dodged a bullet.

That wasn't my main problem, anyway. The problem was keeping it from my friends because I knew they'd make a bigger deal out of it than it was. Dixie, my cousin and obligatory roommate, would continuously offer to cook me stuff. Norelle, our neighbor who never seemed to leave, would offer to egg his car or leave raw meat in his mailbox. And Russell, friend and former fling, would subtly hint at some mood-boosting nookie.

As hilarious as all of this was, I didn't need consoling. I didn't want revenge. All I wanted was an empty apartment, my weighted blanket, and a fresh bag of marshmallows.

Unfortunately, I wouldn't have any time to myself because I could hear their loud asses through the door of my apartment before I even walked up to it. Goodness, these people were *always* here. Now I had to put on my game face.

"Lola!" Dixie loudly greeted me as soon as I walked through the door. She raised her pink glass to me. A lot of her stuff was pink. No comment. "I didn't think you were coming back tonight!"

"Why wouldn't I?"

"I figured you'd be staying over at Orlando's since y'all are leaving for the cabin in the morning."

Oh yeah, we had been planning a romantic Christmas getaway. Weird that I'd already forgotten about that.

"Yeah...there's been a slight change of plans on that..."

"What kind of change?" Russell asked me, looking up from separating his Skittles. Seriously. "He's picking you up on the way out?"

"Ehh." My eyes scanned the room, brightening when I realized it was only the two of them in there. "Oh, Norelle isn't here?"

"Not right now, no."

"Oh, darn." I quickly shut the door and locked it. "Yeah, well, anyway, I'm going to my room. Kinda tired."

"What time are you leaving in the morning?" Dixie asked.

I headed towards my room, running a hand through my locs. "Not sure. But I need a *lot* of rest so if y'all could just...keep the party out here and *not* knock on my door or call me for anything-"

"Hey, hey!" Norelle came bursting through the door, armed with a big box of Krystals and a bag of clanking bottles. "Told y'all I'd be right back!"

My jaw dropped. "How did you do that? I locked the door!"

"Easy. I have a key," Norelle explained, holding it up with a shrug.

I tilted my head at this new information. "And *how* did you get a key?"

"I gave her one," Dixie piped up, all perky and chipper as if that was an okay thing to do. She was already digging into the box of burgers. "I figured since she comes over so much, this way we won't have to get up and get the door for her all the time. Right?"

I loved my cousin. I did. But there was a reason my aunt begged me to let her live with me.

"Yeah, uh...no. Norelle, love ya and all, but if you don't pay rent up in my spot, you don't get twenty-four-seven access to my spot. This ain't *Friends*."

She had the nerve to try to look hurt. "Oh, we're not friends now?"

"That's not what I said and you know it. So save the puppy dog look and hand over the key."

Her jaw dropped. "For real?"

"Come on, Lola, don't be such a stick-in-the-mud," Russell admonished, unloading the wine bottles. "And anyway, somebody should always have an emergency key to your place in case something happens. Norelle is ideal since she's right down the hall. I gave you a key to my place."

"Which I only took under duress and I have yet to use. And my dad already has the only *approved* emergency key. So..." I held my hand out to Norelle, wiggling my fingers expectantly. "Give it up."

"Wow." Norelle marveled, shaking her head. "I thought we were better than that, Lola."

"We're best buds. Now, pick up your little key ring..."

"Fine." She yanked the key off of her penis key chain (she got it at a bachelorette party) and slapped it into my waiting hand. "But don't come crying to me if you forget to turn your water or your stove off or something and your daddy can't get here in time."

"You know we have a landlord, right? Anyway, bye."

"Lola, why don't you hang out for a little while?" Dixie called out as I started again towards my bedroom. "We're having wine and burgers and a Hu-Flix marathon."

Fine, I'd ask. "And what is a Hu-Flix marathon?"

"We take turns watching movies on Hulu and Netflix."

Of course. "Sounds like fun and all, but I wouldn't even be able to hang. I'm pretty wiped."

"Wow, Orlando must have given you some *good* pre-trip lovin', huh?"

Russell groaned, practically stuffing an entire little burger into his mouth.

"It's got nothing to do with that."

"Oh, you're saving it for the trip, huh? I *get* it. I read a lot of romance novels about that very thing. Couples go on a romantic trip and have some amazing epiphany and maybe even an adventure, and then they're totally in love and live happily ever after. *Ooh*, do you think Orlando might propose on the trip?? That would be *so-*"

"We broke up, okay?"

They all looked at me in shock. I hadn't meant to blurt it out like that but I figured if I didn't, Dixie would never shut up and I'd never get to my room.

"What?" Dixie gasped, clutching her shirt over her chest. She was always a little dramatic.

"Girl, are you okay?" Norelle asked, forgetting about her aggravation towards me and rushing over with her arms open. "What did he do? You need me to key his car?"

"I *knew* you were looking kind of drawn lately," Dixie observed. "I thought you were coming down with something but now I see it was just a broken heart. Aww, boo-boo. Let me fry you some bacon."

"Y'all," I held my hands up, amused. "I'm fine. Really."

"Brave face. I totally understand. I'm gonna bake you some brownies, too."

"No, I know what *you* need," Russell piped up, standing as he polished off his second burger and took a swig of wine. He ran a hand down his chest, looking at me in a way that I'm sure was supposed to be sexy. "You need someone to help take your mind off that busta. You know I never liked his ass, anyway."

Norelle fake shuddered. "If she was gonna get sympathy dick, Russell, it would need to be from a stranger she could forget about immediately afterwards, not her friend she had a few romps with back in the day. No, what will make her feel better is if I have a bunch of trash dumped on his doorstep."

I rolled my eyes. Did I know my friends or did I know my friends?

"People," I began inching away from them towards my bedroom, hands up as if blocking them from following me. "I appreciate the concern; I really do. But I don't need anything but to be alone right now. Don't take it personally. So you all just enjoy your booze and your square burgers and your Hu-Flix and don't worry about me. I'm totally fine."

The three of them just stood there looking at me with a sickening amount of sympathy. You would think I was about to fall over at any second.

I continued inching backwards until I was finally in the sanctity of my bedroom. I locked the door, tossed my purse on the bed, and ran both hands through my waist-length locs.

That whole exchange had drained me of what little energy for people I had left.

My name was the only one on the lease of the apartment but ever since I let Dixie move in, I spent most of my time in my room. And since it was decked with my television, desk and laptop, a mini fridge, a cute little shelf from Target for my snacks, a cushy beanbag chair, and plenty of books, I loved it in there. Thanks to my en suite, I could go for days without emerging if I so chose. My friends tended to take offense when I chose to stay in my room instead of hanging out with them, but I hung with them more than I did with anybody else so they really didn't have anything to complain about.

After a long, hot shower, I wrapped up my locs, slipped into something comfy and climbed into bed. I loved my bed. Pillow-topped mattress, weighted comforter, and a gang of fluffy pillows. It was like a hug.

And I curled up in that hug with some marshmallows and *A Different World* marathon for the rest of the night, enjoying my peace.

TWO

"Lola?"

Oh, hell. I didn't even have to look at the time to know it was way too early for this.

Hoping that if I just hushed, Dixie would go away, I burrowed myself deeper under the covers. But unfortunately, Dixie didn't seem to care that I was still asleep.

"Lola!"

Mumbling a *lot* of indelicate language under my breath, I grudgingly sat up. "What?"

"Time for breakfast!"

"I don't want any breakfast."

"Come on! I made you some *cinnamon rooooolls*!"

She sang this like cinnamon rolls were my favorite things on earth. I liked them all right but it was nothing worth waking me up at seven o'clock on a Saturday morning for.

"Lola, get up! We're going to have a great Christmas Eve together!"

That was Norelle. What the hell was Norelle doing there so early?

"Norelle, what the hell are you doing here so early??"

"I crashed on the couch. We drank *so* much wine last night, girl..."

"I'm here, too!" Russell. "You better get up and come on out here before I eat all these cinnamon rolls."

"Eat as many as you want. I'm not ready to get up yet." I flopped onto my back, pulling a pillow over my head.

"Lola, no! We are *not* gonna let you hole up in your room all day," Dixie announced, rapping on my door again. "It's Christmas Eve!"

These people were way too enthusiastic for my state of mind.

I finally threw back the covers and eased off the bed, wiping my eyes as I trudged over to the door. When I yanked it open, the three of them were standing there grinning at me like some kind of creepy painting. I sighed.

"Y'all, I know what you're trying to do and I love you for it. But I really would rather just chill today."

"The thought of you sitting in this room all day watching old sitcoms and eating those nasty marshmallows does *not* sit well with me," Norelle stated emphatically. "We are gonna take your mind off of everything. To hell with Orlando."

"I'm actually not thinking about Orlando at all..."

"Really?" The edge of Dixie's pink hair bonnet rose along with her eyebrows. Norelle and Russell were still in their clothes from the night before while Dixie was in the tank top and shorts she always slept in. "You two were together for over nine months. You loved him, I thought. Didn't you love him?"

"Yes, Dixie. But he wasn't the love of my life. And I don't wanna be with anybody that doesn't wanna be with me, so..."

"He dumped *you*? Damn, I didn't know that. Come on, bring it in," Russell said, holding his arms out and stepping towards me.

I let my head fall back, already tired of this. "Oh my god, please, stop. I said I was fine."

"Of course you would say that!" Norelle exclaimed. "People who have been dumped *always* insist they're just fine and then the next thing you know, they're doing crazy stuff like driving on the wrong side of the road or cutting off their hair-"

"Oh, don't cut off your hair, Lola! I love your locs!" Dixie pleaded. "If my hair wasn't so thin, I'd start some of my own. I'm living vicariously through yours."

"What about mine?" Russell asked her, flipping his own shoulder-length black locs.

"Come on, Russ, you know Lola's locs are *awesome*."

"Yeah, Lola has the *best* locs," Norelle chimed in, looking at me encouragingly. "They should be in a magazine or something. Or a YouTube channel!"

"Yes!"

This was sad. "Do y'all really think I'm so fragile that you need to rave about my *hair* to make me feel better?"

"Is it working?" Russell asked, peering at me. "Or do you need me to do something *else* to make you feel better?"

I had no more words. I just closed the door in their faces and went back to bed.

I don't know how I ended up in a park at a snowman-making contest, but there I was.

Somehow, these people had dragged me out of my awesome bedroom and convinced me to come with them to this event. It was something our community did every Christmas Eve, though it was mostly for kids. Yet there our grown asses were, competing like this was being displayed on national television.

"Russ, it's leaning!" Norelle exclaimed, bumping him aside as he worked on constructing the body. "We're never gonna win this if it isn't straight!"

"I told you, I got this!" Russell insisted, bumping her back out of the way. "Quit hounding me and do what you're supposed to do!"

"I *am* doing what I'm supposed to do!"

"You're doing more fussing than anything."

"I'm trying to win, damn it!"

"Y'all, let's not fight," Dixie pleaded, adjusting her earmuffs. She was the only person I'd ever seen actually wear those. "Our snowman is going to be beautiful. And anyway, the whole point is to have fun, right?"

Norelle and Russell snapped their heads towards her so fast that Dixie actually jumped. I chuckled.

"Uh, *no*," Norelle replied emphatically. Her long black hair hung from under her thick knitted cap and draped over the colorful scarf that was around her neck. "I told you, I'm trying to win."

"Yeah, we got shafted last year and I need to avenge that mess," Russell added, stepping back to peruse his work. He leaned slightly from side to side, then slowly crouched in front of it, his brow furrowed in concentration. He glanced up at Dixie. "You got the tape measure?"

"You people are taking this *way* too seriously," I finally said. I stuffed my gloved hands deeper into my pockets, another shiver rippling through my body. I did *not* like the cold weather. Of all things they had to drag me out to, it had to be something requiring us to stand outside in barely thirty degree weather playing in the snow. "How much longer is this going to take?"

"Maybe if you quit worrying about what time it was and pitched in, we could get this done faster," Norelle muttered, gently sticking the red plastic jewels into the snowman's belly. She had denounced using rocks or coal or buttons. This snowman had to have some sparkle, she said.

"Yeah, Lola, loosen up," Dixie encouraged, coming over and linking her arm through mine. "We're out here together, it's a beautiful day-"

"It's a *cold* day," I corrected her.

"But it's still beautiful," Dixie persisted. She swept her arm around the park. "Look around you; all this snow and the trees and the lights and everyone playing and having a good time. How can you not enjoy this?"

I sighed.

"We just wanted you to help take your mind off things, that's all." Dixie smiled at me, her brown cheeks slightly flushed from the cold. "I couldn't stand the thought of you at home by yourself all day while we came out here and had all this fun."

I didn't even bother saying for the millionth time that I was fine and not pining over Orlando. All I had wanted to do was spend Christmas Eve reading and playing Sims on my laptop, with a big delicious pizza next to me. And I still had to wrap these fools' gifts.

But as much as I didn't want to be in a park making snowmen, I couldn't help but appreciate my friends' concern. They just wanted to cheer me up, even though I wasn't as down as they seemed to want to believe I was.

Telling myself to chill out, I flashed a smile at my cousin and we went over to help Norelle and Russell perfect the snowman. Norelle had brought several props to decorate it, having appointed herself as the leader of this little operation.

"Which wig do y'all think?" she asked, holding a black curly one in one hand and a long-haired blue one in the other. "I couldn't decide..."

"I vote blue," Russell said immediately. "The black one looks cheap."

"It *is* cheap. You think I was gonna buy an expensive wig for this?"

"The blue one is prettier," Dixie chimed in. "That one would stand out more."

"What do you think, Lola?" Norelle asked me.

"I'm gonna go with the majority and say the blue one," I replied, shaping the snow feet that Norelle had decided the snowman just had to have.

"Blue it is." Norelle tossed the black wig back in her bag.

We continued to work together to make our fly snowman, and I was actually enjoying myself. The four of us nitpicked, nudged, laughed, and clowned some of the other snowmen under our breaths as we finished our work. My hands were freezing but by the time we finished, I was actually pretty proud of our snowman.

"*Dope*," Russell assessed, looking the snowman with a smug grin. "Yo, we *got* this, y'all."

"I love all the colors," Dixie praised, snapping pictures. "It definitely stands out."

"Told y'all." Norelle stepped forward to adjust the snowman's boa (yes, boa). "No basic snowmen over here. Folks still using sticks for arms. Weak!"

"Yeah, the mannequin arms you brought are a nice touch. I'm not even gonna ask where you got them. Uh, when is the judging?" I asked, shifting from side to side. My teeth were chattering.

"It's starting now."

The judges went around to the eight or so snowmen, making their observations about each before moving on to the next one. It seemed very unofficial; no clipboards or anything, just muttering amongst themselves what they thought. After they huddled and finally announced us the winners, Russell and Norelle screamed like they had won the lottery.

"I *told* y'all!" Russell hollered, stalking triumphantly around our winning snowman. "Told y'all we were gon' win!"

Norelle and Dixie were holding hands and jumping and dancing around in a circle while Russell continued to loudly proclaim his snowman dominance. I was glad that we won, but I was more ready to get back to my apartment and a big mug of apple cider.

"All right," I finally said, clapping my hands. "Let's get out of this cold and head home so my toes can thaw out. 'Cause I think we're veering into bad form territory now with all this cheering and taunting. Some of these parents are starting to shoot us some looks."

"So?" Norelle shrugged, posing next to the snowman so Dixie could take a picture. "There's nothing wrong with us enjoying our win."

"Sure...but it's getting colder and everyone is starting to pack it in. Plus, I'm hungry."

"No problem. We're going to get pancakes after this."

"Pancakes?"

"Yeah, Toast and Butter is having a special," Dixie replied, snapping a few pictures of Russell flexing behind the snowman. "And I've been *dreaming* about their sweet cream stack."

Toast and Butter was our favorite café in town and usually the idea of hanging out there gorging on their fluffy stacks with homemade syrup would have been a good thing, but my social battery had been draining for the past couple of hours. And I knew my friends; once they got started eating and talking and gossiping and everything else, it'd be hours before we got back home. Just the thought made me want to plop down into the snow.

"Can I get a raincheck, y'all? I'm tired and would just rather go home," I stated. "I'm not all that hungry, anyway."

The three of them stopped and looked at me. "You literally *just* said you were hungry," Russell reminded me.

"You trying to get rid of us so you can go home and call Orlando or something?" Norelle asked, gathering the last of our snowman accessories. She slung the canvas bag over her shoulder. "We're not gonna let you do it. You're coming with us. We're having a fun Christmas Eve, dammit."

My head fell back in sudden exhaustion. "Good grief..."

"Come on, Lola, once you get some of those buttermilk pancakes you love so much in you, you'll feel a lot better," Dixie assured me, dragging me towards the parking lot. "Besides, we're having too good a time for it to end now."

"We can have a good time at home," I insisted, fully aware that I was whining but not caring. "At least, *I* can."

"It's not healthy for you to be alone right now," Norelle replied. "We're your people and we're going to get you through this hard time."

"*What* hard time? There's nothing wrong with me!"

"You got *dumped* right before Christmas, Lola."

"Yes, Russell, I'm aware of that."

"That had to hurt. And as your friends, it's our job to get you through it."

"There's nothing to get through. Why won't you people believe me when I tell you *I'm fine*??"

"You're cranky. You need sustenance," Norelle declared, unlocking the door to her car. I don't know what the hell I was thinking, agreeing to ride with them. I blame it on them catching me when I was still half-asleep.

So I grudgingly tagged along with them to Toast and Butter and sat there in our usual corner booth being held captive while my friends stuffed their faces and yapped about everything under the sun. I was squished between Dixie and Norelle; they wouldn't even let me sit on the end. It was like they thought I'd make a break for it if I did. And after two hours of pancakes and chatter, I can't say I wouldn't have if I had the chance.

My head hurt. I was stuffed. I was tired. The café was full so in addition to the three friends holding me captive, there were plenty more people surrounding us having their own conversations as well as the soulful Christmas music flowing through the air. I couldn't even appreciate the decorations that Ridge, the owner, had put up. The only thing I cared about was getting the hell out of there.

"If I said I had to throw up, could we leave?" I asked before Norelle could launch into another story about which celebrity crush she wished she could meet in the new year.

"Do you??" Dixie asked, concerned.

"Yes. Yes, I do."

Russell narrowed his eyes at me. "You're lying."

"*Try me.*"

"Fine, you big baby." He motioned for the check and I breathed a sigh of relief. Finally.

As soon as we got back to my apartment, I shouldn't have been at all surprised that Russell and Norelle didn't go home. They plopped it on my couch with Dixie, wasting no time debating who was going to be in control of the remote. I made a beeline for my room, ready to fight anybody that tried to stop me.

"We'll be back to check on you in a little bit," Norelle called out, waving a hand as she watched Russell scroll through the TV channels. "You know, since you're so *nauseous* and everything."

"Oh no, no need. Y'all just stay out here and do what you do. I'm gonna ride out the rest of this Christmas Eve in bed."

"*Not* calling Orlando, right?" Dixie verified, hurriedly turning towards me.

"Yeah, girl, don't start scrolling through his social media or anything, trying to see what he's up to," Norelle added. "Remember, *he* dumped *you*. To hell with him."

"I'll try to control myself."

"Let me know if you need me to come back there," Russell called out as I opened my bedroom door. "You know, if you need help relaxing or anything."

I pretended not to hear that. I just closed my door, probably too forcefully, and exhaled. Finally, some peace.

I know my friends meant well. And it was certainly nice to have people that cared enough about me to constantly (*constantly*) check on me and make sure I was okay in what they thought was my hour of need. Maybe they felt especially responsible since I was out with them the night Orlando and I met and they encouraged me to accept his phone number.

Orlando was tall with a nice butt and a sexy voice, yet I wasn't overly interested at first. But he wore me down, and we started dating a couple of weeks later. And it was a cool relationship. I grew to love him. But not once did I look at him and think *forever*. And he clearly didn't think the same about me if he was willing to break up with me after nine months over something so stupid.

That's why I wasn't sweating this breakup. I didn't exactly love getting dumped, but after about an hour I had realized it was for the best and was over it. Though, I guess I couldn't blame my friends for thinking I was more upset than I was letting on, since I might have let them think things between Orlando and I were going better than they were. Things weren't bad, they just weren't super great, but it was easier to let my friends think it was than endure their constant relationship advice. Maybe if I had been honest with them then, I'd be able to enjoy my Christmas in peace now.

My energy was renewed after a long shower and watching a couple of my favorite *A Different World* episodes. Then I finally wrapped my friends' gifts, not being able to help smiling as I listened to them laugh from the living room.

THREE

Christmas day and thankfully there were no knocks on my door or promises of pastries to lure me out of my room. By the time I got up, the apartment was strangely quiet. It was like music.

I checked my phone and saw that Dixie had left me text letting me know she had gone with Norelle and Russell to brunch with Norelle's parents, and they'd be back later. It was so nice of them to not invite me to that.

I went to drop off my dad's gift and hang out with him for a little while before heading back home. When I drove near the park, I stopped for a little while and looked at all the snowmen still up from the contest the day before. I still couldn't believe that I had actually participated in a snowman competition, but it was kind of fun, I admit. Only because my crazy friends were there. They might work my nerves at times but I knew I'd rather have them in my life than not.

After a while of wistful daydreaming, I headed home. I had every intention of baking some thick chocolate chip cookies and watching the Christmas day basketball games in my footed pajamas. What I didn't count on was seeing Orlando leaning against his car near my parking spot when I got there.

"Hey," he greeted me, standing upright when I got out of my car.

"Hey." I stopped a few feet away from him. "What are you doing here?"

"You got a minute?"

"Depends. You here to ask me to pay for the controller I accidentally stepped on?"

He briefly hung his head. "Guess I deserved that." He rubbed his hands together. "I'm sorry for tripping about that; it wasn't really you I was upset about. We had just had that argument, I had a bad day at work and-"

"Took it out on me."

He hunched his shoulders. "Basically."

"Well, good to know." I looked at him expectantly, because I was sure he didn't show up at my door to tell me that. He was holding up my cookies. "Is that it?"

"Can we go inside and talk for a while?"

I sighed and prayed my friends didn't show up any time soon. "We really don't have anything to talk about, Orlando. What's done is done."

"What if I don't *want* us to be done, though?"

"That would be too bad. Because as much as the circumstance and your timing sucked, you actually did me a favor. We could've wasted years together even though I think we both know we're not each other's *one*. We never even talked about anything long-term."

"That doesn't mean I don't want it, Lola."

"Oh, so you can see me as your wife one day? You can deal with a life of my – as you call it- *antisocial behavior* and *social ineptitude*? Remember how upset you got every time I wanted to leave a party before you did or didn't feel like going out?"

"So I like to hang and go out and stuff. That doesn't mean we're incompatible."

"Orlando," I shook my head, "Let's just leave well enough alone. I don't need to be with someone who tries to make me feel bad for being the way I am. And that was you. So I'd rather not waste time trying to force something that isn't meant to work. I'm good."

"Wow." His brown eyes searched my face, as if trying to verify my sincerity. I looked right back at him, unflinching. "I, uh...I guess I'd better be going, then."

"Yeah."

"I still want you to have your gift." He produced a wrapped box from behind his back, holding it out to me while he averted his eyes.

I started to tell him to keep it, but decided that would be stupid. So I just took it and stepped back.

"Thanks."

I didn't have one to give to him in return. That sucker was already headed back to the company I had ordered it from.

"Merry Christmas, Lola," Orlando said, finally getting back into his car.

"Same to you."

I stood and watched as he left. I was still marveling that he had shown up at all when my phone chimed with another text from Dixie; she, Norelle, and Russell were going to some party and she asked if I wanted them to come pick me up.

I do not. Have fun.

I unlocked the door to my apartment and headed inside, glad I was going to get to enjoy my Christmas the way I wanted.

Wooing the Introvert

ONE

There was so. Much. PINK.

It was clear that Dixie had been in charge of the decorations. She adored the color and got everything possible in some shade of it, if she could. I felt like I had fallen into a bowl of Valentine's candy.

"Lola, you want some more wine before I kill the rest of this bottle?"

I looked over at Norelle, who was holding the near-empty chardonnay bottle and wiggling to the music blasting through her apartment. She was having a Valentine's Day party, which meant lots of wine, food, and flirting. And that we could finally hang in her apartment, for once; she was at my place so much I was going to Venmo her a request for a cut of the rent.

"I'm good; you can go ahead," I replied, the words barely out of my mouth before she had the bottle turned up to her lips. I just chuckled and shook my head, popping another meatball into my mouth and venturing back into the sea of people crowding her living room.

"You drunk?" Russell asked me, seemingly appearing in front of me from nowhere. He peered down at me curiously.

"No...why?"

"You're still here. I figured you would have snuck out by now."

Sucking my teeth, I playfully nudged his chest. "Hush, Russell. You act like I *never* party with y'all. Hell, I went to that New Year's Eve shindig. I can even say I had a good time."

"But you left early, though."

"I was there for three hours! Y'all were trying to party 'til dawn and I can't hang like that."

"Can't hang like what?" Dixie, my cousin, asked, appearing beside Russell. Her face was a little flushed and I wasn't sure if it was from the higher-than-necessary heat in the room or from her wearing herself out with her non-dancing. She was really not good at it.

"We were just talking about how Lola left the New Year's Eve party earlier than we did," Russell told her, sipping his beer. "And that I was surprised she was still here now."

"You know Norelle would pitch a whole fit if Lola snuck out of here. But you're having a good time, though, aren't you, Lola?"

"Yeah," I replied sincerely. "Even though Norelle thinks she's slick with this little theme she's got going on. Y'all know how she's been complaining about not having a man for weeks. That's why she made this a single's event."

"Really?" Dixie looked around, taking renewed stock of the room. The men slightly outnumbered the women, which I still don't know how Norelle managed to pull off.

"Yeah, cuz. If she had a man, this would probably be a couple's only shindig and you, me, and Russell would have to be pretending we're in some kind of polyamorous thing."

"But that wouldn't be a *couple*, though."

"Semantics."

"Yeah, she *would* try to have us doing some mess like that," Russell agreed, shaking his head. I could tell he had just gotten his locs retwisted; they were styled in some kind of intricate pattern and gathered in a low ponytail, and he didn't know how to do that stuff himself. He winked at me. "Not that I would have a problem acting like your man, Lola."

Good grief. Russell was forever flirting with me. We fooled around years ago when we were in college but it never went any further than that, yet he still somehow enjoyed acting like he wanted to go there with me again. I loved Russell dearly but he was neck-deep in the friend zone.

"Uh-huh," I droned with a good-natured roll of my eyes as I sipped my cranberry juice. I lightly bobbed my head to the music as I turned to scan the crowded room. Everyone was mingling and dancing and drinking and having a good time, and I couldn't help but love the good vibes. I could admit this was better than camping out in my room watching Black love movies and snacking on marshmallows.

"My *peeps*!" Norelle exclaimed, jumping between me and Dixie and damn near knocking us over as she plunked her arms across our shoulders. "What's *uuuuppp*..."

"Yep, somebody's tipsy," I observed, amused, as I touched the bun my long locs were wrapped into on top of my head. "You hooked up yet?"

"Not yet but I've got some prospects. The last guy I talked to was so fine I almost kicked the rest of y'all out."

"I would've understood that. I guess."

"Yeah, I just *bet* you're looking for any excuse to get up outta here," Norelle replied, her eyes narrowed. "But if you sneak outta here, Lola, I'm telling you now, I won't come over to your place for a month."

"And that's supposed to be a deterrent?"

"I think somebody over there has a taste for a tall glass of hot coffee," Russell commented, eyeing a woman across the room as he gulped a swig of his beer.

"Who drinks *tall glasses* of hot coffee?"

"Don't hate, Lola, you had your chance."

"What the hell-"

He had already gulped down the rest of his drink and headed across the room. I just shook my head and went to see if there were any meatballs left.

By the time I had finished raiding Norelle's small kitchen, Russell was talking to the hot coffee lover, Norelle was grinding against someone who I'm sure we'd be hearing around later, and Dixie was cornered by a guy with a back broad enough to play a movie on. Since all of my friends were coupled up and preoccupied, I figured it would be a good time to start easing my way towards the door. I really had been enjoying myself but after a couple of hours of loud music, alcohol, and a room full of people that I in large part didn't know, I needed a break.

I slipped off to the bathroom, squeezing between all the dancing bodies. After relieving myself and savoring the few moments of relative quiet, I went off to find Norelle to let her know I was heading out. Hopefully she'd be too focused on the gentleman she was dancing with to care.

My friends were all still doing their thing, so I grabbed another bottle of cranberry juice as a parting gift and started easing towards the door. I tried to wave to Norelle and Dixie over my shoulder, but they weren't paying me any attention. As much as they had been drinking, I could probably get away with saying I'd told them I was leaving and blaming the alcohol on them forgetting.

"Whoa!"

"Oh!" I stumbled backwards, and a pair of strong hands quickly grabbed my elbows to steady me. When I looked up to see who my noble savior was, I was amazed to actually be taken aback by the cuteness.

"You good?" he asked.

"Yeah...I'm fine, thanks."

He pulled his hands back. "Heading out, huh?"

"Oh...yeah. I think I'm about partied out."

"I'm not too far behind you. I told my boy I'd show my face but I really want to get back home and watch the game."

The small smile came all on its own. "The Heat game? Yeah, I hated that I was missing that, too. Um, how do you know Norelle?"

"My friend works with her. He told me to come through, try to meet somebody. Though I wasn't expecting to see so many dudes..."

"Yeah, Norelle kinda screwed y'all with that one," I chuckled. "This whole thing is glaringly self-serving."

"It's whatever," he shrugged. "I only agreed to come so I wouldn't have to keep hearing about how I never get out of the house. Wasn't planning on staying too long, anyway." He looked at me. "I bet I sound pretty boring, huh?"

Why was I so intrigued? "Nah, I wouldn't say that. What's your name?"

"Jackal."

"What?"

"I'm kidding." He chuckled, revealing a nice set of teeth. "I'm John."

"Hmm. Jackal actually would've been more interesting."

He cracked up. I grinned.

"And you are?" he asked when he calmed down.

"I'm Lola."

"First person I've met with that name. That means I'll remember you."

Oh my god, I was blushing. It was probably a good idea to get away from this man, though my feet didn't move when I mentally ordered them to.

"Well, that's...that's flattering..." I managed to say, suddenly a little nervous. My tendency to get awkward around men I was attracted to was rearing its unwanted head, I see. "Thanks, I mean...I hope you do. If you want."

He leaned a little closer to my ear. "I wouldn't be mad if we kept in touch after this," he informed me. "No pressure, though."

I looked at him.

"I guess I shouldn't assume that a lovely lady like yourself is available," he continued. "My bad if I'm stepping on any toes, here."

No toe-stepping. I was recently single after my ex dumped me for something stupid so that was absolutely not an issue.

"No, you're good," I finally spoke. "I'm unattached and wouldn't be mad at that, either."

We exchanged flirtatious smiles as we each pulled out our phones, exchanging the digits. Out of the corner of my eye I could see Russell watching us, but I didn't acknowledge it. I'm sure the barrage of questions would be coming soon enough, even though I had no such plans to grill him about the woman shaking her tail in front of him.

"So...I'm gonna head out," I said to John after another few moments, moving so my back was to Russell.

"I can walk you to your car. I'm on my way out, too."

I debated whether I wanted to let him know that I lived just one floor up. He was cute and all but I wasn't sure I needed him to know where I lived already.

"I didn't drive, actually," I revealed.

"Oh okay, you got an Uber or something?"

"Nah...I live in the building. But-"

"Say no more; I get it," he held his hands up. "You're not ready to let me know where you live yet. Totally understandable."

I breathed a little sigh of relief that he didn't trip. "Really?"

"Of course. You don't know me. It's just good sense to be cautious."

"Thank you for not taking it personally."

"It would say a lot about me if I did. Come on, I'll walk you to the elevator."

We made easy conversation as we strolled to the elevator. Part of me wasn't quite ready for us to part ways yet, and I felt a little silly that I didn't know how to let him know that without sounding thirsty. Then I was silently admonishing myself for thinking that would make me sound thirsty at all. It had been a while since I was this nervous around a man.

I ended up riding with him down the lobby, not quite ready to leave his company. He smelled delicious and now that we were out of Norelle's loud apartment, I could appreciate just how buttery-smooth his voice was. I could listen to him read cleanser ingredients and be transfixed.

"How long have you been growing your locs?" he asked me, as we lingered in the lobby. He clearly wasn't in a big hurry to leave and I wasn't in a big hurry for him to leave.

"Oh wow...it's been about twelve years, now," I replied after thinking about it for a minute. "Had a big 'fro before this. Started locs because I was no good at styling my hair and got tired of all the maintenance; it was either loc it up or cut it off."

"I think you made the right choice. I bet they're hot when they're down and framing your face."

My cheeks flamed as I smiled at the compliment. "That's sweet of you to say. They're down around my waist by now. I love 'em."

"I can see why." He checked his watch and I felt myself deflate a little bit, preparing to hear him tell me he had to leave. I still wasn't ready for that but at least he had my number already; I'd like to think I'd hear from him again.

"Say, Lola..."

"Yeah?"

"I know it's getting kinda late but...you wanna go and grab something to eat? We can hit up Toast and Butter for some pancakes; it's probably busy but I don't mind waiting..." He looked at me with those creamed coffee-colored eyes of his and I felt myself melt a little bit. "Well, I wouldn't mind if you were there with me."

No way was I turning that down. And since there was no smooth way of saying that I needed to run upstairs for a panty change because he had gotten me inexplicably horny from a pancake invitation, I just grinned and took hold of his outstretched arm.

"Lead the way, sir."

TWO

"Lola!"

I figured this would be coming sooner or later. Norelle's voice was almost shrill as she screamed from the other side of my bedroom door.

Now usually, the fact that she was there so early and making so much noise would have irked me. But this time, I just chuckled as I finished putting on my ankle boots and went to open the door.

"Norelle, what a surprise," I droned, leaving her and Dixie standing there as I went over to my closet.

"You have some explaining to do, miss thing."

"Do I?"

"Since *when* do you stay out all night??"

"Since *when* do I have a curfew?"

"None of us knew where you were, Lola," Dixie chimed in. "You disappeared from the party without saying goodbye to anybody. And Russell said you left with some guy."

"Which he was *not* happy about, by the way," Norelle added.

I frowned slightly as I pulled a sweater from my closet. "What? Why should he care?"

"I don't know but he was really salty about it. That's the main thing he fussed about, other than having to stay and help clean up after I got tired of all those people in my house."

"Well, whatever," I shrugged, slipping into the sweater and fluffing out my locs. "He'll get over it."

"So who was it you left with?" Dixie asked me. "You have to admit, it's not really like you to just go off with some random guy. We were just a little worried, that's all; especially since you didn't answer our calls and barely responded to our texts."

I looked at my cousin and neighbor-friend and sighed. They looked genuinely concerned.

"Okay, that wasn't cool of me," I acquiesced. "I should've at least let you know I was leaving the party. But honestly, I was enjoying John's company so much that I wasn't really thinking about much else."

"John, huh?" Norelle smirked at me as she folded her arms. "So that's who you left with. Y'all must have really hit it off since you still weren't here when I walked Dixie up here once everybody left."

"Walked her up here? I thought you would've been up under that dude you were dancing so much with last night."

"You act like it was our second date or something. I don't give it up that quick."

"Oh, how soon we forget Vegas..."

"Hey! What happens in Vegas doesn't *count*!" Norelle exclaimed, pointing a finger at me. "And quit trying to change the subject. I should be asking if *you're* the one that spent the night under somebody since you stayed out all night."

"Yeah, Lola, I'm a little surprised at you," Dixie said, resting a knee on my unmade bed. "That's totally out of character for you. Is this your way of trying to get over Orlando?"

"Lord," I rolled my eyes as I gathered my locs into a ponytail. My ex Orlando and I had broken up almost two months earlier and Dixie was still acting like I was pining for the man, when I really didn't think of him at all until one of them brought him up, which I wished they would stop doing. "I am *over* Orlando, Dixie, despite what you seem to want to believe. John invited me to get something to eat after we left the party and then we ended up talking all night. I really wasn't thinking about what time it was."

"Are you going to meet him *now*?" Norelle asked as she eyed me putting on my small hoop earrings. "You usually work at home and you're in here getting all cute and stuff."

"Oh my gosh...I have to go into the office for a meeting, Norelle. Not everything revolves around men." I worked as a web designer and loved that it allowed me to work alone, for the most part. But occasionally I did have to go and interact with people. Unfortunately. "Hopefully it doesn't take all freaking day."

"Uh-huh. So you're not seeing John again? I have to give you props, girl; he's mad cute."

I couldn't help but smile proudly at that, which was ridiculous because he wasn't my man. But I admittedly didn't hate the thought of him holding that title. "No arguments here. And to answer your question, yes, I'm seeing him again."

"Oooh! I hear ya, girl, trying to get your *groove* back! Does he have any brothers?"

Laughing as I double-checked my laptop bag to make sure I had everything, I gently nudged Norelle and Dixie towards the door. "Two, actually, but they're both married. And speaking of work, shouldn't both of y'all be at your own jobs?"

"I took the day off," Norelle replied with a wave of her hand. "I already knew I'd be in no condition to deal with those kids today."

"And I have the late shift," Dixie informed with a huff. She was a bartender, of all things. "Which I hate. The later it gets, the crazier folks get."

"You get good tips, though," I reminded her, locking my bedroom door. "And you're the one who wanted to pour drinks instead of using your Psychology degree. I've gotta get out of here, y'all. I'll see you later."

"If you plan on not coming home and hanging out with this John dude again, could you at *least* do us the courtesy of letting us know this time?" Norelle called out as I headed for the door. "Just so we know what's up."

Geesh, I thought I was done checking in with folks when I moved out of my dad's house. "Yeah, whatever."

John had texted me a few times throughout the day, and each time brought an automatic grin. I felt like a goofy teenager with her first crush.

It had been a while since I crushed on someone this hard this fast. Not even with Orlando. I actually wasn't all that interested in him at first; he had to grow on me. But John had my attention right off the bat. The smooth maple brown skin, thick dark eyebrows, and lips that I was already fantasizing about kissing were intriguing enough, but his personality had me equally enamored. Once I got over my initial awkwardness, we fell into this smooth, easy rapport that I hadn't had with anyone else. It was nothing for us to sit in his car for hours and talk after we left Toast and Butter the night before; the time just sped by. And yet I *still* wasn't ready to leave him when I did.

I was just getting back from my meeting when John texted and asked if it was okay to call, winning himself even more points. Talking on the phone wasn't always my favorite activity.

After giving him the go-ahead, my phone rang mere seconds later and there I went grinning again.

"Hey," I greeted him.

"Hey, Lola. Your meeting go okay?"

"Ehh. It was a work meeting."

"I feel you. You got some more work you need to do?"

"Yeah, I have to put some time in on this project I've been working on. The deadline is this weekend."

"Understandable. Well, whenever you have some time, I'd like to see you again. You've been on my mind since last night."

"Yeah? When were you thinking about?" I asked, grinning harder. "Seeing me, I mean."

"Just let me know when you can fit me in. I know you need to handle your business, so I can be patient."

Him being so accommodating just made me want to find time for him as soon as possible. "Well, how 'bout I put a few hours in on this project and then hit you up? If it's not too late."

"Doesn't matter how late it is for me. I'm down when you are. Just let me know."

After talking for a few more minutes, we ended the call and I grabbed my things, heading into my building with a little more spring in my step than usual. I was actually whistling. The music stopped, though, when I saw Russell waiting beside my door.

"What are you doing out here, Russell?" I asked as I approached.

"Dixie isn't here and I don't have a key."

"You don't have to keep reminding me that I won't give y'all keys. It's not like it's going to make me change my mind. What do you want?"

"We need to talk, Lola."

"About?"

"Can we go inside first? I've been waiting out here for a half hour and I need to use the bathroom."

"Ugh," I grunted as I unlocked the door, hoping this wasn't about some foolishness. Russell rushed to go relieve himself as I deposited my bags in my room and kicked my shoes off. I met Russell back in the living room, who was already eyeing me as I joined him on the couch.

"Okay, what's going on?" I asked him.

"What's up with you, Lola? Leaving the party last night with some random like that? *And* spending the night with him? Since when do you do that kind of shit?"

I reared back at his words, frowning. "Why are you coming at me like I did something wrong? And not that I have to explain myself, but I did not *spend the night* with him, at least not in the way you're implying. Even if I did, though, I can do that, Russell; I'm single and I'm grown."

"I know how old you are. But I've been right here all this time and you keep treating me like a joke, yet you're willing to entertain some stranger. And I'm not gonna act like I don't take that personally."

"Where in the world is all this coming from? Last night you were hitting on some woman and telling me I'd missed my chance, now you're acting insulted that I met someone else?"

"Well, you're always acting like you're not interested..."

"Interested in *what*? You and I both know you just flirt with me for the hell of it. We haven't been together like that in years."

His dark eyes looked at me piercingly. "Whose fault is that?"

The seriousness in his expression was throwing me off. If he was messing with me, he was putting on an Image Award-worthy performance. But I didn't get the feeling he was joking. "What are you saying, Russell?"

Before he could respond, Dixie burst through the door laden with grocery bags.

"Oh, thank *god* you're here, Russell!" she exclaimed, blowing some of her brown hair from her face. "Can you help me get the rest of the bags from the car?"

"Yeah." Russell gave me another look before he stood from the couch. I just sat there dumbfounded, still trying to process the exchange we just had.

Dixie was babbling on and on about something that happened at the grocery store, and didn't seem to notice when I wandered into my room and closed the door. That weird exchange with Russell was clouding my mind already, and I didn't have the capacity to absorb whatever random story Dixie had that day. She always came home from the grocery store like she was coming from some life-altering expedition.

After several more moments of trying to analyze my conversation with Russell, I decided to put it out of my mind. That was all totally out of the blue and I had to believe that he was just upset about something else and projecting it onto me. Because I refused to believe that he had any actual feelings for me all of a sudden. Why would he wait so long to say anything about it, if that was the case?

Whatever. I didn't have time to worry about Russell's mood swings. I needed to get to work so I could meet John later.

"I hope you like cupcakes."

I had taken a chance and let John come over, since Dixie was at work and Norelle and Russell thought I was still working. Dixie wouldn't be home for hours and the door was locked, so we'd have some privacy.

"Of *course* I like cupcakes," I confirmed, grinning as he slid the familiar butter yellow box closer to me on the coffee table. "Especially when they're from Pure Sugar."

"I'm glad because I was having a hell of a time trying to decide between these and the banana pudding cookies. Peaches said that was a new thing on the menu."

"Ohh! You couldn't have lost either way. I love when she adds new stuff." Peaches was a local who had opened the Pure Sugar bakery a couple of years earlier after she got laid off from the custodial job she had worked for almost twenty years. Her son Tango helped her run it. Her calling card was that she insisted on using real butter, lard, sugar, all that. She always said if you wanted diet desserts, go somewhere else.

"I got an assortment since I wasn't sure what you liked," John informed me, opening the box. "You're not allergic to anything, are you?"

"Nope. You know, you're making major strides, bringing me desserts. My sweet tooth is epic."

"Good to know." He winked at me as he nudged the box my way. "Help yourself. Ladies first."

We noshed on cupcakes in comfortable silence, exchanging flirtatious glances and smiles as we licked frosting from our lips and fingertips. Every time I saw his tongue ease out of his mouth, it made something warm shoot through my body.

Damn. Watching a man eat cupcakes was turning me on.

"Let me get that for you," he muttered, gently wiping a bit of frosting from the corner of my mouth with his thumb. His eyes bore into mine, and I had to bite my lip to avoid taking his thumb between my lips and sucking. I noticed he took his time removing his hand, and my head slightly leaned into it, not being able to resist. His skin was so warm and he smelled like sugar. I ached to get closer.

We each put whatever was left of our cupcakes onto the coffee table without taking our eyes off each other.

"I wanna kiss you," he told me. "But if it's too fast-"

"It's not," I interjected, not caring how eager I sounded. "I want you to."

He looked at me before dropping his gaze back to my lips. "Good."

He gently grabbed the back of my neck and leaned in. I exhaled when our lips met, feeling my heart speed up as we deepened the kiss immediately. Fireworks were exploding all over my body, and I grabbed the front of his jacket, bringing him closer.

In no time, we were full-on making out. My back was braced against the back of the couch as John hovered over me, held in place by my hand clamped on the back of his neck. He moaned gently against my lips, his hand tightening on my hip.

"Is this a bad time to confess how into you I am already?" he asked, nuzzling my cheek.

Before I could tell him it was a perfect time, I heard the doorknob jiggle and then three loud knocks.

"Lola! You in there?"

"Son of a *bitch*!" I grumbled, my head falling back in frustration. Just like that, I wished I had taken John up on his offer to go to his place.

"Who is that?" John asked me, looking towards the door then back at me with concern.

"It's Russell."

"Lola! We saw your car outside!"

"And Norelle," I added grudgingly. "Friends who apparently don't have anything better to do than bother me."

"You need a minute?"

"I wish I could say they'd go away if we pretend like we're not here, but I know better than that." I straightened my clothes and ran my hands down my face before standing and going over to the door, fully intent on sending these nosy people on their way. "Just a second."

Hurrying to the door, I opened it just wide enough to glare at my pests. "What the hell do y'all want??"

"You done working? We wanted to check out this movie but I didn't pay my Netflix bill," Norelle informed me. "Can we watch it here?"

"No, you can't. I'm busy."

"What does it matter? You'll be in your room, anyway; we won't bother you," Russell persisted.

I sighed, frustrated. "Why can't y'all go to *your* house, Russell?"

"Your place is closer."

"Well, too bad. You can't come in here."

"Why not?"

"Because I'm entertaining."

"What??"

"Ooh, you got John in there?" Norelle hissed excitedly. "Say no more, girl. Sorry to interrupt. Come on, Russell."

"Wait a minute!" Russell frowned at me, unmoved when Norelle tried to pull him away. "You told us you had to *work*, Lola!"

"I did. And now I have company so you two need to roll."

Russell was trying to peek over my head into the apartment. "Why don't you let us meet your *company*, then?"

I glared at him. "I don't know what's up with you, Russell, but I'm not feeling this attitude you've got going on. You need to chill out."

"Yeah, Russell, you're acting like Lola is cheating on you or something," Norelle chuckled. "If I didn't know better, I'd think you were jealous."

Russell was looking at me with some strange look in his eyes. He almost looked...hurt. Then he glanced at Norelle before storming off down the hall.

"Don't worry about that, girl," Norelle dismissed with a wave of her hand. "He'll be all right. I think he's just in his feelings 'cause that woman he met at my party lied about not having a man."

I shook my head, though I was a tiny bit concerned about Russell. He was acting strangely and I had a feeling there was more to it than what Norelle thought.

But I wasn't about to let it ruin my evening with John. After Norelle walked off, I closed and locked the door.

"Everything okay?" John asked me.

"Oh yeah, it's fine."

"Your boy sounded pretty upset," John observed as I rejoined him on the couch. "If you need me to leave so you can go talk to him, I understand."

"No thank you," I retorted, pushing his jacket from his shoulders. "All I need you to do is bring me those lips again."

He smiled, biting his lip as I pulled him closer by the front of his shirt. "Yes ma'am."

THREE

After my fourth date with John, he asked if I wanted to make things official, and I wasted no time agreeing. I'd been craving that invitation more than I craved sweets.

And I *always* craved sweets.

I really felt I had hit the jackpot with John, and (I can't believe I'm saying all this corny stuff but I mean it) I was happier than I'd been in years. He made me tingle and wish and daydream.

And it was nice that at least *two* of my friends were happy for me.

"Do y'all know what's up with Russell?" I asked Norelle and Dixie as we headed back to the car after leaving the mall. Norelle just had to add to her ridiculously large shoe collection. She could do that but couldn't pay her Netflix bill. An observation I kept to myself. "He's been avoiding me lately, seems like."

"I don't know; he's been acting funny," Norelle replied as we got into her car. "Every time I ask what's wrong, though, he just says he's dealing with some stuff he doesn't want to talk about."

"But at least he still hangs out with *y'all*; he acts like he doesn't want to be around *me*. Ever since I started seeing John, he's been acting like I wronged him some kind of way. He didn't even want to meet him when we all hung out last week."

"Lola," Dixie turned to me from the passenger's seat, looking thoughtful. "I'm gonna tell you something that Russell probably doesn't want me to tell you."

"What?"

"Well...you know how he's always flirting and hinting around about the stuff you two did in college? He's not just saying that to be saying it. He actually wants you."

My jaw dropped. "He said that??"

"Yes. A while ago. He made me promise not to tell you and I honestly forgot about it for a while, but when you got with John and Russell started making himself scarce, I remembered."

"He didn't say anything about that to *me*!" Norelle exclaimed. "Why would he just tell *you* that?"

"Norelle, come on; you're not the best at keeping secrets."

"I can keep secrets fine! There's *plenty* of stuff I haven't told y'all!"

"Aww, like what?" Dixie asked, suddenly looking hurt.

I cleared my throat. "Can we stay on topic, please? Russell seriously said that he wanted me for real? He wasn't drunk or anything?"

"No, he was totally sober," Dixie confirmed. "I thought he was just messing with me at first but he insisted he was serious. He just didn't know how to come out and tell you."

So that's what it was. That explained Russell's behavior, but now I didn't know how to handle knowing about this.

"Wait a minute, though," I spoke up after a moment. "Russell didn't act any differently when I was with Orlando. And he and I were together for like nine months. What's the difference with John?"

"Maybe he can tell that you're more into John than you were into Orlando," Norelle suggested. "You've been spending just about *all* of your free time with John, barely hanging out with us. With Orlando, it wasn't like that. Not to mention, you've had that newly-sprung glow, grinning and laughing at stuff that isn't funny. If you're not in love with that man already, you're on the express train to it. Dixie and I totally get it but Russell...not so much."

"Wow," I marveled, sinking down in my seat. The *last* thing I wanted to do was hurt Russell, or lose him as a friend. But I damn sure wasn't about to give up a good man that I was really into just because Russell dragged his feet with telling me about his feelings. Though I don't even know what I would have said if he *had* told me.

"So what are you gonna do?" Dixie asked as we pulled out of the parking lot.

"Not sure," I mumbled, chewing my lip thoughtfully. I reached into my purse and pulled out a bag of marshmallows, mindlessly popping one into my mouth.

"Oh my god. You carry those in your purse?"

"Of course. I don't carry such a big bag for fashion reasons."

"Lola," Norelle glanced at me through the rearview mirror, "You're gonna have to talk to Russell."

"And say what?"

"Girl, I don't know."

"You're such a wealth of advice."

"Just let him know that your relationship with John is very important to you, but that doesn't mean that you love Russell any less as a friend," Dixie suggested. "I'm sure he'll understand that."

"Eventually," Norelle added.

"And who knows," Dixie continued, "Maybe you and John won't even work out."

"Gee. Thanks, Dixie." I rolled my eyes.

"No!" Dixie exclaimed, realizing how her statement sounded. "I only *meant* that you and Russell could go back to normal if you and John split up, that's all. Then everything would be fixed."

"Stop talking, girl," Norelle admonished. "Even if something happened and Lola and John split up, she would still know what Russell wasn't ready for her to know. She can't exactly pretend you didn't tell her that."

"True," I agreed with a sigh. "I *do* need to talk to Russell and straighten this out. I just have to figure out what the hell I'm gonna say."

Turns out I didn't have a lot of time to do that, because we saw Russell's truck in the parking lot when we pulled up to me and Norelle's building.

"Good luck," Norelle whispered to me before we all got out of her car. She and Dixie went on into the building while I hesitantly went over to Russell's truck.

He unlocked the door and I climbed into the passenger's seat, plunking my hobo bag into my lap.

"Hey," I greeted.

"Hey." He wasn't looking at me.

I wasn't sure how to proceed here. Should I let him know I knew about what he told Dixie or try to get him to admit it himself?

He cleared his throat. "So...I guess I should let you know why I've been acting like I have been."

Never mind.

"Okay..."

"I've been trying to...work up the nerve to tell you something. Ever since you and Orlando broke up, I haven't been able to make myself come out with it..."

I could tell this was hard for him so I let him take his time.

"Lola...I've wanted us to give a relationship a shot." He finally looked at me. "Like, for real. Ever since we messed around in college, I've liked you as more than a friend. But, you never seemed like you wanted to take it there again, so I just turned the flirting into a playful thing. Wasn't trying to get my face cracked."

"Russell..." I turned towards him, looking at his handsome face. I swear his skin was like Belgian chocolate; I've always thought that was one of his best features. "I wish you had told me, just so I could know what the deal was. Even if I didn't feel the same way-"

"You didn't." His voice was flat.

"Regardless, maybe if I had known, we could've avoided all this tension we have between us now. For real, I had *no* idea that you carried any kind of torch for me after all this time. And I'm sincerely flattered. But I hope you can understand that I'm just not in the same place."

"Because of *John*," he grumbled, looking out the window.

I pursed my lips. "Even *before* John came into the picture, Russell. But now that he is, I don't want our friendship to be damaged because of it. I love you and want you in my life just like you've always been; crashing in my living room and eating up my food and using my streaming services more than I do."

The corner of his mouth twitched like he was trying to hold in a smile. Headway.

"Russell," I gently shook his arm, trying to get him to look at me. "Come on, work with me, here, dude. I can understand why you've been acting like a jackass recently. But hopefully as my friend you can find some way to be happy for me, because I'm *really* into John and want to see where things can go with him. And I don't want you to feel like you have to stay away every time he comes around, 'cause he's going to be around a *lot*."

"Umph."

"Russell."

"Okay, okay," he sighed, throwing up his hands and looking at me. "I get it. And I'm sorry for getting in my feelings without telling you what the deal was; that wasn't cool. If this John makes you happy and shit, then I can find some way to be cool with it."

I chuckled, gently nudging him. "I appreciate that."

"Norelle said the reason y'all probably clicked so hard was because John is another introvert like you are."

"We have that in common, among other things. Plus..." I couldn't resist smiling. "He *wooed* me. And I've never been wooed like that."

"*I* tried to woo you, Lola," Russell stated, sinking a little in his seat. My smile faded slightly. "But I clearly didn't do it the right way."

I worried that the little bit of progress we'd just made had disappeared, but Russell quickly shook off his sullen expression.

"I have to admit it *is* nice to see you smiling instead of walking around like a sourpuss all the time and closing yourself off in your room like you don't want to be bothered with anybody," he teased, reaching over to nudge my shoulder. "Dude must have unlocked some kind of secret code."

"Shut up and give me a hug, Russell."

He leaned over and we shared a hug best we could from our seats. He gave me a good-natured kiss on my cheek as we parted, looking at me tenderly.

"So, we're okay?" I asked him.

"Yeah, girl." He smiled, tweaking my chin. "We're good."

"I'm glad to hear that 'cause I have a date with John later and I want you two to finally meet."

"Can I have a key to your crib?"

"Hell no."

"Worth a shot. Fine, I'll meet your man and try not to rough him up too much."

"Don't play."

"You got any snacks? That *aren't* sequestered in your den of solitude?"

"You know we *keep* snacks. Plus, Dixie started some jambalaya in the crock pot before we left this morning. Said she was gonna make crescent rolls to go with it."

"Aww snap, you should've led with that," Russell exclaimed, quickly pushing his door open. "And I hope John is taking you somewhere to eat 'cause I ain't savin' a damn thing."

I just chuckled as he hurried into the building without me. That was my boy.

The Introvert Roast

ONE

His warm hands slid along my shoulders and started massaging. My smile was automatic.

"You're spending the night, right?" he asked with his lips close to my ear. "You've spoiled me, letting me get used to waking up to you."

I leaned my head back slightly, enjoying his pleasantly manipulating massage. "You've already hit pay dirt but I'll let you keep saying stuff like that."

John chuckled and kissed my cheek before letting his lips slide down to my neck. My eyes fluttered closed. "I'll say damn near whatever you want as long as you stay."

He turned me to mush when he said stuff like that, and I'm sure he knew it. No complaints here, though. We were barely eight months into our relationship and I still blushed and got all tingly around him like I did the night we met at my friend Norelle's Valentine's party.

"I'm not going anywhere," I assured, the seriousness of my statement getting lost in the moans from him sucking my neck.

"I'm gonna hold you to that, you know."

"Go ahead," I urged, giggling as he hopped over the back of the couch and pulled me to him. He was always all over me and I loved it. "As long as you don't mind a little reciprocation 'cause I surely don't want you going anywhere, either."

"You're officially stuck with me."

"Promises, promises."

He turned my face to his and laid one of the good ones on me. I so loved kissing him; it was like I was addicted to his lips.

"Hey, there's something I wanted to run by you," he said when we stopped acting like a couple of horny teenagers.

"Okay..."

"What do you have going on for Thanksgiving? You gonna be hanging out with your dad or Norelle and Dixie and 'nem?"

"I'm not sure, actually," I replied, pushing my locs off my shoulder. "Dad mentioned something about going out of town for the holiday this year with his brothers. And my friends haven't really mentioned any plans yet. Why?"

"Well...your presence has been requested at my parent's house, if you're up for it."

"Wow." I tucked my socked foot underneath me and chewed on my lip. "Dinner with the folks, huh?"

"Yeah. I know meeting the parents can be a big deal so if you don't feel like you're ready for that yet, I get it. No pressure."

I appreciated that because I *was* a little on the fence. I was crazy about John, and I knew I'd have to meet his parents eventually since my status as his woman was locked in, if I had anything to say about it. But I hadn't thought about doing it any time soon.

"Who all is gonna be there?" I asked him. "Are we talking family flood or..."

"Nah, babe, my family isn't even all that big. It'll be my folks, my brothers and their wives, my sister, if she decides to show up, and probably a few more people; aunts, uncles, a couple of cousins."

"You're not making this sound like not a lot of people."

"Say the word and we'll just kick it here. Or whatever you wanna do."

"Oh, so they can blame me when their little pookie bear doesn't show up for Thanksgiving? I'm not trying to start out in the doghouse."

"My folks aren't like that, Lola," he assured with a chuckle. "Mama is as chill as I am. Dad can be a little...*energetic* at times, but he's one of the nicest guys you'd ever wanna meet."

"Energetic, huh?"

"Why am I not surprised that you honed in on that one word?"

"Do you *really* want me to go?" I asked, peering at him.

"Of course. But if you don't feel up to it, it's fine. Believe me, I love my family but I don't always have the energy for 'em, either. My folks aren't going anywhere; you can always meet them another time."

I kept chewing my lip thoughtfully.

"Hey." He clamped a hand on my thigh and moved closer to me. "Don't stress yourself deciding this. I won't take it personally if you say no, trust me."

"Really?"

"I'm secure in how you feel about me, babe. And I also know that being in a room full of my family for the first time on a holiday can be a lot."

He was right; I *did* feel like a lot. Just the thought of being put on display for John's family during a holiday dinner made my palms sweat a little bit.

But John was important to me, and I knew he wanted me there, regardless of all the outs he was giving me. And I'd have to meet his parents eventually so there wasn't much sense in putting it off.

I looked at him and couldn't help but smile. He was so damn cute. Those creamed coffee-colored eyes always did something to me. Not to mention his dark wavy hair, the sexy earring he wore, those lips...

There was something I had to know first, though.

"Are we gonna have to be over there all day?" I asked him.

"*Hell* no. My limit is three hours, whether you go with me or not."

"Sold."

"If you're gonna be spending all your time over at John's, you might as well give me and Russell some keys," Norelle announced as soon as I walked through the door of my apartment the next day. "Always leaving Dixie here by herself. You know she can't handle living alone."

"I still live here. And Dixie wouldn't be alone, anyway, since you and Russell never seem to leave." Shaking my head at the usual sight of my neighbor Norelle, friend Russell and cousin-slash-roommate Dixie, I adjusted my overnight bag on my shoulder. "What reason have you concocted for being here *this* time?"

"We're talking about what we're gonna do for Thanksgiving," Dixie piped up from her spot on the floor, where she was coloring in a coloring book. I wish I was kidding. "Since my parents moved out of state and your dad is going out of town..."

"And I'm not trying to be around my ignorant family any more than I am the rest of the year..." Norelle muttered.

"And my cruise plans tanked..." Russell spoke up, then paused and grinned at me. "Get it? Cruise? *Tanked*?"

I rolled my eyes. "Yes, Russell, you're a regular Kevin Hart. Now what were you-"

"If you're gonna compare me to somebody, make it an OG like Martin Lawrence. Or better yet, Eddie Murphy. I look more like Eddie Murphy."

"What? Russell, you look *nothing* like Eddie Murphy," Norelle scoffed. "You're both Black men; that's the *only* thing you have in common."

"We're both of the dark chocolate variety."

"So?"

"Women love that. And neither of us has ever had any issues getting the ladies."

"How come you couldn't get Lola, then?"

Dixie gasped, I groaned, and Russell was looking like he wanted to kick Norelle off the couch with his size twelves.

"You didn't have to go there," he growled, frowning hard.

"Yeah, Norelle, that was unnecessary," I agreed, hoping that her little dig didn't push Russell back into the funk he was in for a while after I got with John. Apparently he had been harboring a crush on me that he didn't know what to do about and I messed everything up by falling for somebody else. It had taken us a while to get back to normal after that; there were times when Russell still acted like he didn't want to be around John. But I saw he tried to be cool with our relationship and I appreciated the effort.

"What?" Norelle was actually trying to look like she didn't know what the big deal was. "Oh come on, Russell knows I'm just messing with him. Don't be so sensitive."

"Why don't you try being a little *more* sensitive?" Russell muttered, scooting further away from Norelle.

"Russell, are you seriously-"

"*Anyway*," I interjected before they went back and forth forever, "What were y'all talking about regarding Thanksgiving, Dixie?"

"We were going to go hiking in the morning, then come back and have a nice long brunch." Dixie already looked excited about all this. "Then dessert while we watch all the football."

"What time are you gonna be good to leave, Lola?" Norelle asked me. "We know how you like to sleep in on holidays."

"Oh. Yeah, about that..." I went to put my bag and purse in my room, or as others might call it, stalling, "I'll probably be staying over at John's that night."

"We figured that. You're always over there. We can just kick things off when you get home, though."

"Hmm. Okay, John invited me to his parents' house for Thanksgiving so...I won't be able to go with y'all."

They all whipped their heads towards me. "You're gonna be over there *all day*??" Russell exclaimed.

"Enough of the day."

"Wow."

"Damn, Lola, I'm happy for you and everything, but you could at least leave *some* time for us," Norelle grumbled. "We were here before he was."

I shook my head. "If I'm not mistaken, Norelle, you and Dixie just started dating people, yourselves."

"Yeah, so?"

"Why won't y'all be with them?"

"Girl, please, it's *way* too early in the game for family holiday meet-ups. I just started kicking it with Drone like a month ago, and Dixie and her boo Ryan are barely three months in."

"Ooh, did I tell you guys about how Ryan would come wait with me until I got off at the bar and keep me company?"

"Yes!" Russell immediately exclaimed, holding up both hands. "Yes, you did. *Many* times."

"He is so *sweet*!" Dixie gushed, grinning as she started doodling pink hearts along the back of her coloring book. "He refuses to let me leave there at night by myself, even with security there. And he got me this adorable hoodie!"

We knew. She had told us *that* story a hundred times, too. Not to mention the fact that she wore that hot pink hoodie damn near every other day.

"That's awesome, cuz," I made myself say. Dixie was supportive of me and John so it was only right that I give some of that back, especially since her new man seemed like a nice guy. Hopefully she'd come down off that new-boo high soon enough, though, 'cause I didn't know how many more times I could listen to these same stories.

"But Ryan has to work on Thanksgiving, anyway," Dixie added, pouting.

"Aww," I leaned down and patted her shoulder. "Well, y'all, look on the bright side."

Norelle looked at me. "What's the bright side?"

"I was never gonna go hiking, anyway."

They all sucked their teeth at me as I chuckled my way to my room.

Nature called in the middle of the night and after I took care of that, I wasn't able to go back to sleep. I usually slept like a log so I felt a little out of sorts being up at three in the morning.

Wandering into the living room, I half-expected my friends to be camped out on my couch but surprisingly, the room was empty. I went to the kitchen and mindlessly opened the fridge, even though I didn't want anything in there. Same with the cabinets. There was a strange feeling in my gut and I started to grab my go-to snack of choice, marshmallows, but realized I didn't even want those. This was after eating like six of them, though.

"Lola?"

I sat up from where I had sprawled on the couch to see Dixie's curious and concerned expression. "Hey. How was work?"

"It was okay. Got a lot of tips." She removed her coat and hung it in the closet. "Are you all right? What are you doing up so late?"

"Wish I knew. Had to use the bathroom and couldn't get back to sleep."

She parked it on the other end of the couch, pulling out her phone and typing a message.

"Letting Ryan know you made it home, huh?"

"Yeah." She finished sending her message and looked over at me. "You sure you're okay? You seem like you've got something on your mind."

"Do I?"

"Yep. You always bite your lip or twirl your locs around your finger when you're thinking about stuff."

I hadn't even realized I was doing that. "I'm fine."

"Do you think you're nervous about meeting John's family?"

My brow quirked and I started to automatically say no, but maybe that wasn't so ridiculous. It *had* been clouding the back of my mind more and more ever since I agreed to it. "Could be, yeah. I mean, I'm not exactly excited about it."

"I'm sure it won't be that bad. John is a great guy; I bet his family will be, too. You don't have anything to worry about."

"I guess. I'm just not used to feeling like this and it's throwing me off."

"Why, though? You think something bad is gonna happen?"

"I just feel like *something* is gonna happen. Not sure if it's gonna be bad or not."

"Lola. You know how you get when you know you're gonna be meeting new people. You start dreading it, thinking the worst, anticipating all this negative stuff-"

"That's *not* what I'm doing."

"Sounds like it to me. And if I know you -and I do- you're going to build all this stuff up in your mind so much that come Thanksgiving morning, you'll have come up with a hundred reasons why you can't or shouldn't go to John's."

Hmph. She didn't have to be so accurate about that.

"Just go in thinking positively," Dixie continued, correctly surmising that I wasn't going to admit she was right out loud. "Meet his folks, eat some turkey, hang out for a little bit, then you and John can spend the rest of the night alone."

I was already looking forward to that part.

And I knew I had a bad habit of agreeing to stuff that required me to socialize and then looking for any viable excuse to get out of it afterwards. Part of me was hoping a pipe would bust or the roof would cave in or something at John's parents' house (of course, when no one was home) and we wouldn't have to go over there.

But since I knew that probably wouldn't happen, and me flaking for no good reason wouldn't be a good look, I'd just have to go and hope for the best. I mean, really, how bad could it be?

TWO

"Just three hours, right?" I confirmed as John and I pulled up to his parents' house.

"Tops."

"Okay but just so you know, one minute longer and you owe me a foot rub."

"In that case I'll have us here 'til midnight so I can get all in you."

My jaw dropped briefly before I broke out into a big grin. I loved when he got all smooth-nasty like that.

"Don't make me jump you in this car."

"Don't tempt me." He grabbed my chin and brought my face to his for a kiss. "Let's go on in and get the party started."

One time I really, *really* hoped that was just an expression.

John held my hand as we snaked between the cars that filled up the driveway. I glanced down at my outfit and hoped for the hundredth time that I looked all right; I had changed clothes four times before settling on a wine-colored off-the-shoulder sweater, light jeans, and knee-high boots that matched my sweater exactly and I'd only worn once. I could only hope foot discomfort didn't become another issue.

We'd barely rung the doorbell before we were faced with this big, burly man who swept us both up into a bear hug.

"It's about time!" he practically yelled before putting us down. When I finally got a look at him, I immediately knew it was John's dad. It was like a vision of what my man would look like in thirty years.

"Dad, we're not late," John reminded him with a chuckle and a slap on the shoulder. "It's only five until one."

"Well, we've been looking forward to you two getting here ever since you said you were bringing your lady friend." His dad turned and grinned at me, giving me the once-over. "She's a looker, son."

"That she is." John winked at me. "Dad, this is Lola."

"Lola! *Love* that name!" He snatched me into another hug. John said his dad was energetic but he didn't warn me about all this strong hugging. "Great to meet you, sweetheart!"

"Same here," I managed to say, even though he was squeezing me like he was trying to get me to squeak.

"Uh, Dad," John muttered, tapping him on the arm. Clearly this was a regular thing.

"Oh right, sorry." Father John quickly pulled back and took my hand in his. "You can call me Big Poppa."

I glanced at John, unsure if I was supposed to take that seriously or not. "Um...is there a second option?"

He threw his head back and howled laughing. At least he had a sense of humor. "I *like* her, son!"

"I knew you would," John winked at me. When Original John turned to yell something to someone in another room, John leaned over and whispered, "You can just call him John Sr. He hates being called 'mister' anything."

"Got it. But he *was* kidding with the Big Poppa thing, right?"

"Wish I could say he was."

"Three hours, huh?"

John smirked at me and patted his dad on the shoulder. "Where's Mama and everybody else? We're not the last ones here, are we?"

"Oh no. We're still waiting on a couple of people. Your mama is in there in the dining room."

John grabbed my hand and headed that way, acknowledging people along the way but thankfully not stopping at every person that spoke to him. We entered the dining room to find a tall woman with short gray hair putting plates on the table. When she saw us, she smiled.

"There you are," she greeted, and I couldn't help but notice how smooth her voice was. Definitely a voice made for radio. Or GPS tracking apps. "I was wondering if you two would show up."

"How are you, Mama?" John asked as he wrapped her in a hug.

"I'm great. Glad to see my baby boy." She lovingly rubbed his back and turned her eyes to me. They were the same creamed-coffee brown as John's. "You must be Lola."

I plastered on a smile. "Yes, ma'am."

"It is so nice to meet you. Just call me Marilyn." She grinned and held out her hands, which were nice and warm when I put mine in them. "John has been going on and on about you for months. I'm glad to be able to put a name with the face, finally."

I couldn't help but grin upon hearing that John had been gushing about me to his mama. He had already told me he was closer to her than anyone else in his family so I was flattered by that.

"It's nice to meet you, too," I reciprocated. "Thank you for having me."

"Oh, you're more than welcome." She gave my hands a little squeeze before releasing them. "You just make yourself at home. We're going to be eating in just a few minutes; John's sister is running late. Again."

"Oh, Jessa's coming?" John looked surprised. He moved to help his mother with the plates but she waved him away. "I didn't think she was, from what she was saying the other day."

"I never know what that child is gonna do," Marilyn muttered, setting the plates and straightening the silverware. "She might show up, she might not. But we're going to start eating in five minutes whether she's here or not."

Music to my ears. I was hoping this wasn't a thing where nothing started until every single person that was expected to show up actually arrived. Not to be stereotypical but I had yet to go to a Black family gathering where *everyone* was on time.

John took me into the den where the other people were and gave a general introduction, but thankfully didn't try to introduce me to every individual person in there. There were at least ten people and there was no way I was going to remember all those names.

"You good? Want a beer or something?" John murmured to me, sliding an arm around my shoulders.

"As tempting as it is to get buzzed, I'll pass."

"You wanna sit down? We can squeeze onto the loveseat over there."

"I'm good over here. If I'm in the midst of everybody like that someone might start taking me through 'the list.'"

"The list?"

"You know...the 'so, what do you do?', 'did you grow up around here?', 'how many siblings do you have?', 'stovetop or oven mac and cheese?' That kind of stuff."

"Ahh, I get it. Though I know you're playing with that last one. Everybody knows anything other than baked mac and cheese is trash."

Just when I was about to agree, the front door opened and since we were standing in the entryway between the foyer and the den, John and I automatically turned to see who was coming in. I didn't blink when the two women entered but I heard John curse under his breath, something he didn't do much of.

"What's wrong?" I asked, alarmed.

He looked at me apologetically. "I'm sorry about this, babe."

"Sorry about what?"

Just then, one of the women shrieked when she saw John and rushed over to throw herself into his arms. From the way she tried to practically straddle him, I guessed this one wasn't his sister. I hoped not, at least.

"Well, this is new," I observed, watching this little reunion.

John shot me another apologetic look before gently pushing the woman off of him and stepping back. "Hey, chill out with that," he grunted to her. "Not cool at all."

"I'm just so happy to see you!" the woman exclaimed, trying to hug him again. He held up his hand, stopping her.

"Why are you here?" He looked to the other woman, who was watching them with an amused expression on her face. "What the hell, Jessa?"

"Hey, she asked if she could come with me since she didn't have anything else to do. What was I supposed to say, no?"

"Actually yes, that's exactly what you were supposed to say." John sighed and glanced at me. "Babe, this is Chandra. My...ex."

I blinked. Suddenly a hike wasn't sounding so bad.

"Interesting," was all I could manage to say at the moment. I cut my eyes at John and resisted the urge to tell him that his three hours had just been sliced dramatically. At least the heffah didn't try to shake my hand and lie about how nice it was to meet me. She just eyed me like I was eying her.

"And this is my shady sister, Jessa," John continued, nodding to the other woman. She had short locs that were super neat and I usually would have commented on, but for the time being, I didn't like her. So I didn't care what her hair looked like.

"I'm not trying to start anything, I *swear*," Jessa insisted, looking back and forth between me and John. Her eyes still looked mischievous, though. "I *totally* forgot that Mama mentioned John would be bringing his girl with him."

"Right." John didn't buy that any more than I did.

Chandra must have realized she was still giving me the stink eye when she suddenly snapped out of it and plastered on a smile. "I didn't know John had moved on already. I'm trying not to feel some kind of way about that."

"Chandra," John sighed, "We broke up *two years ago*, not last week. And we haven't talked in months."

"Well, that's because you quit taking my calls, remember?" She shot an accusatory glance at me, like that was my fault.

Well, I guess in a way, it kind of was. Oh well.

"Whoa!" John Sr.'s voice boomed from behind us. He rushed over and gave Chandra one of his over-zealous bear hugs, which she gleefully accepted. "I didn't know you were gonna be here! Marilyn! Come look who showed up!"

And just like that, damn near everybody that had been in the den flooded to the foyer to see the (not so) surprise guest, with someone stepping on my toes in the process. I had to move way off to the side, practically in the corner, while everyone gushed over this woman who used to be in a relationship with my man. I know they *just* met me and all, but that was a little insulting for them to do that in my face like that. I already felt forgotten.

"Lola!" I heard John's voice over all the commotion.

He wedged his way through his yapping family members, came over to me and grabbed my hands, looking contrite.

"I'm *so*, so sorry about all of this, babe," he expressed. I believed him, but that didn't make me any less annoyed. "I swear to *god* I didn't know she was gonna be here."

"Well, apparently she's a welcome addition, with how happy everyone is to see her," I replied in a lowered voice, not trying to hide the snippiness. "I thought you told me you broke up with this woman and no longer spoke to her."

"I did and I don't. But I only tell my family so much of my business, so they don't know about all that. They just know we split and I refused to talk about her afterwards."

"Great plan. Now this is twice as uncomfortable."

"Do you wanna leave?"

"Yes, I wanna leave. But me running out of here two seconds after your ex shows up won't reflect well on me, and I know that."

"I'm not worried about what anybody thinks, Lola. I don't want you to be uncomfortable."

"Well, we've already established that ship has sailed, haven't we? So I'll just have to deal with it."

"No, you don't *have* to deal with it. I don't want to be around Chandra any more than you do. It's not like I was talking about putting you in an Uber while I stayed here to get reacquainted. We can *both* be out. You're the only one I'm worried about, Lola."

He looked so sincere I couldn't help but let my frown melt a little bit. I knew this wasn't his fault.

"I appreciate it," I told him, reaching up to caress his cute face. "And while I would love nothing more than to get out of here, I can suck it up for the time being. I came here to start getting to know your family and if that means I have to share space with your ex for a while, so be it."

He leaned in and kissed me, and we kinda got lost in the moment and forgot where we were. By the time we remembered and parted lips, all eyes were on us. I jumped like someone had thrown a scarecrow at me.

John shook it off quicker than I did and started towards the dining room, my hand in his. "So...let's eat, huh?"

I tried to tell myself to chill out as everybody sat down to dinner. So John's ex was there; so what. So she couldn't seem to keep herself from gazing at him and glaring at me. Big deal. So damn near everybody in John's family seemed to be still enamored with her and barely paid me any attention. Whatever.

Try as I might, though, I couldn't quite quell my uneasiness. It was already a big deal for me to be there with my man's family at all, but meeting his family *and* his ex all at once was way more than I signed up for. I had to stop myself from continuously checking the time.

"What do you do, Lola?" some woman whose name I couldn't recall asked from across the table. One of John's aunts, was all I knew. "And I *love* your hair. It's gorgeous."

"I certainly appreciate that compliment, thank you. To answer your question, I'm a web designer."

"Oooh, girl, you already won points with me. The only thing I can do with a computer is turn it on."

"Or ruin 'em," the man next to her muttered. "You're way better at *that*. Wasting water on my laptop, cracking screens, dropping it on the floor-"

"Nobody asked you all that."

"So...Lola, is it?"

She was talking to me. The ex was talking to me.

"That's me." I tried to keep my face even as I speared a yam.

"How long have you been seeing John? I figure it can't be *that* long, since no one has mentioned you."

John started to say something, but I placed a hand on his arm. "We've been going strong for a while now." She didn't deserve exact details.

"Hmm." Chandra glanced at John, then back at me. I took note of her shoulder-length brown hair, dangly earrings, and glittery top. Full face of makeup, too. Homegirl was really doing it up for a dinner at her ex's house. "Are you two...serious?"

"As the plight of those starving babies in Africa. I'm not going anywhere."

A few people chuckled. John smiled as his hand gently squeezed my thigh under the table. "That's right. And neither am I."

Chandra's expression faltered a little and her accomplice Jessa wasted no time jumping in. "Where did you two meet?"

Damn, wasn't there anything else to talk about? "At a party. He saved me from embarrassment when I almost fell on my behind."

"*You* went to a party, John?" Jude, one of his brothers, asked in surprise. "Whenever *I* invite you to those you always flake out."

"Yeah, well," John shrugged. "You've gotta catch me on the right day."

"And you two met and fell for each other and the rest is history, right?" Jessa asked, clearly being a smart-ass.

"If that's how you want to put it, sure," I replied amusingly. "We definitely clicked right off the bat. I guess you could say I knew I had a good thing and wasn't going to do anything stupid to mess it up."

I might've been looking right at Chandra when I said that. And by the way her eyes tightened and she clanked her fork to her plate, I guess she didn't appreciate it.

John cleared his throat, apparently seeing it, too. "How 'bout we stop grilling Lola and talk about something else?"

More like roasting, I thought to myself.

"Are we making you uncomfortable, Lola?" Marilyn asked. "We definitely don't want to do that."

"Aww, she's not uncomfortable!" John Sr. spoke up, waving off the notion with one hand and jamming a huge forkful of dressing into his mouth with the other. "We're just trying to get to know her, that's all. I'm sure she knows it's all love over here."

No, I don't *know that. 'Cause it's not.*

"Still, though," John persisted, giving me another under-the-table thigh squeeze. "Y'all firing off question after question at her can be a little much. I brought her to meet my family, not be interrogated."

"Yeah, he's not wrong," Jimmy, the other brother, assured. John told me he was the sibling he got along with the most. "Especially since neither my nor Jude's wives got the same treatment the first time we brought *them* here."

"Thank *god,*" the lady sitting next to Jude - his wife, I presumed – muttered under her breath.

"Fine, we'll chill out," Jessa agreed. "One last question, though, Lula-"

"Hey Jessa...it's *Lola,*" I quickly interjected, looking straight into her scheming eyes. Though I had no doubt she knew full well what my name was. "My name is Lola."

"My bad. *Lola.*" She cleared her throat. "Did you know that Chandra and John almost got *engaged*? Had their whole futures planned out; how many kids they were gonna have, where they were going to build a house, start a business together, what city they'd retire in. Have you two even *discussed* anything like that?"

"Some. We'll definitely be discussing more of that as we continue to grow together."

"You sound pretty sure of that. What makes you think John won't dump you like he did Chandra?"

"Because *I* won't cheat on him like Chandra did."

The collective gasps might've been funny in any other situation. The horrified expression on Chandra's face certainly was, though.

John probably hadn't wanted me to divulge that bit of information but we'd just have to argue about it, if that's what he wanted to do. He wasn't the one constantly being swatted at like flies at a cookout.

Meet-the-family time was a wrap for me. Even though I kinda wanted the rest of my ham, I needed to get out of there. It was just too combative and uncomfortable and I wasn't going to keep subjecting myself to that, whether they were John's family or not.

"Thank you all, but I need to head home now," I announced, putting my napkin on top of my plate and standing. "I have to make sure my constant houseguests haven't eaten all my stuff."

Without waiting for a response, I left the table, ignoring John Sr. calling my name and Marilyn telling him to leave me alone. Apparently, she could understand why I didn't want to be around them anymore. At least that was something.

"Lola!" John was right on my heels as I stormed out the front door. "Lola, hold up!"

"John, if you're mad at me for spilling the beans about what happened between you and Chandra, then you'll just have to be mad," I told him, holding up a hand. "I was sick of being treated like I had no business being there with you and I figured that was the only thing that would shut the Drama Twins up."

He just looked at me with an expression I couldn't quite read. Taking this as a bad sign, I sucked my teeth and tried to unlock the door to his car, looking at him pointedly. He just pursed his lips and unlocked the door, opening it for me with a slight frown on his face. And I got into his car with a less-slight frown on mine.

What a fun Thanksgiving.

THREE

"You want me to take you home?"

He finally spoke after we had spent most of the ride from his parents' house in silence. I glanced over at him. "That depends."

"On what?"

"On if you're in your feelings about what I said back there."

He started to say something, then stopped himself. "I don't want to leave things like this but if you'd rather go home, I'll respect that."

He and I both knew that we wouldn't get the privacy we wanted if we went back to my place, since Dixie, Norelle, and Russell were probably back from their hike and pigging out in dessert mode by then. The three of them were invasive enough but hyped up on sugar, they were twice as bad. Even if John and I locked ourselves in my room, they'd keep finding excuses to knock on the door.

And I *definitely* wasn't in the mood to go in there alone and have to answer a bunch of questions about how things went.

"We can go to your place," I mumbled, my face turned towards the window.

Back to the silence we went.

As soon as we got to his house, John went to change clothes and I kicked off my boots. The stubborn part of me wished I could go home and stew about how the day turned out but the more mature part knew I needed to deal with it now. I still wasn't sure if John was upset or not and if he was, exactly what he was upset *about*.

When he came back to the living room in a t-shirt and sweats, I had to ignore how tasty he looked and remember how annoyed I was.

"Babe," he sat down next to me on the couch, close but not touching. "Can we talk now?"

"Not sure what there is to talk about. My meeting your family was a major fail."

"I'm sorry about that..."

"I know it's not your fault. You didn't know your ex was gonna be there." I cut my eyes at him. "*Did* you?"

"No! I had no idea Jessa and Chandra were even cool like that."

I turned to him. "Why didn't you tell your family the real reason the two of you broke up?"

"Because I didn't want to have to keep talking about it over and over," John replied with a sigh, leaning back on the couch with an arm behind his head. "Depending on the person, I'd either get asked a ton of questions about what happened, comforted into oblivion, or try to be convinced to give her another chance. And finding out about what she did was bad enough; I didn't want to deal with all that, too."

"I can understand that. But if it's been a couple of years, I'd think enough time has passed..."

"Does my family seem like the type that can let things go?"

"Valid point. But...and I hope you don't take this the wrong way...but is there *any* part of you that didn't tell them because you were embarrassed about getting cheated on?"

John looked over at me with mild surprise. I guess I wasn't supposed to point that out.

"It's not a fun thing to admit," he finally said, letting his head fall back on the cushions. "Especially since she didn't seem to think it was that big a deal. She actually suggested I look at it as a 'slip-up' and forget about it."

My jaw dropped. "She really said that?"

"Swear to god. And we had been together for three years by then. Apparently that meant different things to us; for me it was a sign of major disrespect but for her, it was some kind of insurance that she could get away with whatever. I ended it the same night she told me about it."

"Wow, John." I rubbed his leg. "And I thought getting dumped for stepping on a game controller was bad."

He chuckled. "Almost equally as stupid." His hand covered mine as he gazed at me. "I'm sorry today was so bad for you."

"Is the fact that I have no desire to be around them again any time soon a deal-breaker? Your mother was all right but other than that-"

"I get it." He sat up and gathered my hand in both of his, looking at me intently. "I just don't want you to think that what happened today changes anything with us. At least, *I* don't want it to."

Relief hit me like a hard shove. Part of me had been afraid that this would become a big issue between us. We'd certainly had some arguments during our relationship but this was involving his family; I knew that was another level.

"I don't want it to, either," I replied, turning towards him. "But...how is this gonna work? Me not being around your folks that much?"

"Are you saying you never want to see them again *in life*? This was just *one* unpleasant incident, that's all, babe. It'll get better. And I'll be sure to make it clear how I expect them to treat you from now on."

"Will they listen to you?"

"They're not monsters, Lola," he chuckled. "Yeah, my sister can be childish and my dad has no clue how loud he is half the time but they mean well. You just need to get to know them, individually. I know they're gonna love you as much as I do."

Damn it. I didn't want to grin so hard at that but I couldn't help it. "I'm sure I will. But I don't think your sister *meant well* with the crap she was saying earlier."

"I'm not gonna try to defend her on that. She was straight-up out of line and *will* be hearing about it from me. But now that they know the real deal about Chandra, trust me, they won't be so sweet on her."

"You sound sure about that."

"I'm absolutely sure about that. Cheating is not something they get down with. When Jude stepped out on his wife a few years ago, they put him through the wringer for months. Or should I say, *we* did, 'cause I damn sure joined in."

I chuckled.

"We might not be perfect but we take relationships seriously." He slid an arm around me and pulled me closer, looking right into my eyes. "And I'm as serious as I can be about you, Lola."

"Aww, babe..." I blushed, my head falling into the crook of his neck for a moment before looking back at him. "I'm so serious about you, too."

"Yeah?" He tipped my chin up with his finger, eyeing my lips before meeting my eyes again. "*How* serious?"

I was eyeing his mouth, too. And grabbing the front of his shirt. "Damn serious. Now come put those lips on me."

He nudged me onto my back, his hands already sliding under my sweater. "Yes, ma'am."

I surely had a *lot* to be thankful for.

I, Take Thee Introvert

ONE

I wasn't much of a sap, but even I could appreciate the romantic vibe in the air.

"It's such a nice night," I observed, my eyes roaming around us. There were a few people wandering around but for the most part, my man and I had the area to ourselves. Always ideal.

"It really is." John's thumb stroked my hand. "Love clear nights like this. And it's pretty warm for this time of year."

"I've never been one for star-gazing, but it's hard not to appreciate the view tonight." I looked up, then at my ridiculously-cute man, smiling. "And I don't just mean what's up there."

He looked at me and grinned, pulling me to him. "Keep flattering me like that and I might stick around for another year." His lips touched mine. "Happy anniversary, babe."

"Happy anniversary." I stole another kiss. "With your cute self."

Blushing and smiling, he ducked his head. You'd think he'd be used to that by now because I was forever proclaiming his cuteness. "You know I could've taken you somewhere a little nicer tonight. I love Toast and Butter, but..."

"That's where we had our first date. Call me a romantic."

"You?"

"I'm enough of one." I led him over to one of the wrought-iron benches that were scattered around, snuggling close to him once we were seated, his arm tight around me. "Too bad we can't just spend the night out here."

"I can turn on some nature sounds when we get back to my place, if you want."

"I guess that'll do."

"I'm glad you suggested we come out here, babe. This is actually better than what I had in mind."

I looked at him curiously. "What do you mean? In mind for what?"

Taking a moment as if gathering his nerve, he slowly retracted his arm from around me, languidly rubbing his hands together for a moment before reaching into his pocket. He slid a tiny bit away from me as he put something on the bench between us.

His eyes were on the ground as he nervously fiddled with the cuff on his jacket. "That's for you."

Since it was dark outside, the little black box wasn't totally visible; I had to feel around for it a little. When I did, my heart started racing a little bit, but I immediately told myself to calm down. It was probably some earrings or a bracelet or something. There had been one I'd mentioned liking a couple of weeks before, and he was certainly enough of a sweetheart to remember that and surprise me with it.

When I opened the box, though, there was no bracelet. There was a ring.

"Oh..." I breathed, emitting some kind of sound that I was too stunned to be embarrassed about. When I looked up at John, his warm brown eyes were on me, giving me one of those looks that always had me feeling like a romance novel heroine. "Is this...are you..."

"I'm asking you to marry me, Lola." He turned to me, taking my free hand in his. "If this year with you has shown me anything, it's that I want a whole lot more of 'em. You mean *everything* to me. And the more I think about a life of coming home to you and movie nights with your legs in my lap and lazy weekends together, the more I want it. I want you and me to be a permanent thing."

I was choked up. And I didn't get choked up. Unless someone died.

"John..."

"Will you be my wife, Lola?"

I might've been blinking back tears, but I was grinning, too. So hard my face was starting to cramp.

"*Hell* yes," I whispered, because that's how it came out. My locs fell over my shoulder as I continued to nod vigorously. "Absolutely, *yes*."

With a relieved smile, he pulled my face to his and kissed me, both of us quickly forgetting that we were sitting in the middle of a park. Several moments passed before we finally tapered off and he eased the ring box from my hand.

"Thank you for saying yes," he murmured, sliding the oval-cut blue diamond ring onto my finger.

"Thank *you* for not doing this in public."

We shared a chuckle as he touched his forehead to mine. "I know my woman. Us practically alone in a park is a loophole."

I touched my hand to his face before bringing it within my eye line, marveling. "Wow..."

"You like the ring?"

"I *love* the ring."

"You know your friends are gonna freak when they see it, right?"

My hand dropped. "Thank you for inviting me to stay at your place tonight."

"That's where I was taking you, anyway."

"Well, let's go, because I'm ready to celebrate this news with you." I stood, holding onto his hand. "Especially since we both know that once people hear about it, all hell is gonna break loose."

"Between your friends and my family? You don't have to remind me." He stood, linking his fingers through mine as we headed for the car. "I'm not in a particular hurry to broadcast it."

"Well, let's just keep it between us for now, then. It'll be our mischievous little secret."

"So you're gonna take the ring off every time you go home?"

"I was thinking of just not going home, period."

"Even better. We'll just enjoy this on our own for now and...deal with all of them later."

"You sure you don't wanna just elope tonight?" I asked him, only half-joking.

"I actually wouldn't be mad at that. But my mama would be pissed at me indefinitely. And you too, probably."

"Yeah, I don't want that. She *is* my favorite out of your family, after all."

"Because she doesn't talk your ear off like the rest of 'em?"

"That's exactly why."

"All right, well," he sighed as he opened the passenger door of his car for me. "We'll worry about that later. For now, it's just me and you."

"That's how I like it."

Of course, it was only a matter of time before John and I had to come out of our little bubble. We'd been holed up at his house, and since my job as a web designer and his as a I.T. specialist allowed us to work from home most of the time, we were perfectly fine with staying to ourselves, cooking together or ordering takeout, and enjoying a whole *bunch* of engagement consummation, which was now a thing.

But I knew I had to go home eventually, especially since my cousin Dixie, and friends Norelle and Russell were whining about me never being there. It was funny how they were acting like this was something new; there were plenty of times where I spent stretches of time at John's, because he was my man and I wanted to be up under him more than I wanted to keep Norelle and Russell out of my business and my refrigerator.

Don't get me wrong; I loved my friends dearly. And it wasn't like I didn't want to hang with them *at all*; I did. But they were still having a hard time accepting that things were just different now.

And if they were fussing now, there was no telling *how* they'd react to finding out that I was engaged. I'd like to think they'd be happy for me but...that remained to be seen.

I pulled up to my apartment building, sighing as I grabbed my purse and overnight bag from the backseat. It made me smile to think that it would only be a matter of time before I didn't have to cart stuff back and forth anymore because I'd be living with John, but I couldn't cross that bridge 'til I got to it. And along that bridge was our family and friends and wedding planning; not terrible things in and of themselves, but really, John and I just wanted to get married and start our lives together without a ton of fuss.

Resisting the brief urge to pocket my engagement ring, I headed up to my place. My friends would find out eventually and the longer I waited to tell them, the more grief I'd get about it. So no sense in putting it off.

Surprisingly, the apartment was empty when I entered. Relieved, I went and stashed my stuff in my room before texting John that I made it home safe. I was getting my dirty clothes ready to put in the wash when I heard Dixie's voice. Then Norelle's. Should've known.

I set the laundry basket I was holding on my bed and went out to the living room. The two of them were laughing about something or other, then turned and saw me.

"Hey!" Dixie exclaimed, grinning. She rushed over to hug me. "I didn't know you were coming back today."

"Yeah, you've been over at your boo's house so much we thought you moved out on the sly and didn't tell nobody," Norelle added, coming over for her own hug, then a playful bump to the shoulder. "We would've checked to see if your stuff was still here, but of course you always keep your door locked."

"Well, you can thank yourself for that, Ms. I'll-just-borrow-Lola's-jacket-without-asking," I reminded her.

"That was *one* time!"

"One time is enough. I wouldn't put it past y'all to be congregated on my bed watching my TV if something ever happened to the one out here."

"We wouldn't do that," Dixie immediately insisted.

"We'd at least call and let you know first, if we did."

"Thanks for being honest about that, Norelle." I eyed the door behind them. "Where's Russell? He's not coming by here?"

"Yeah, he got hung up at work; he'll be by later on, he said."

"Hmm." I wanted to tell them all at the same time, but now that they were standing in front of me, I didn't want to wait. Plus, I was tired of keeping my hand in my jacket pocket.

"Why, what's wrong?" Dixie asked.

"Oh, nothing's *wrong*." I pulled my left hand from my pocket and held it out to them. "So...this happened..."

They both looked down at my hand and gasped. In the next second, Dixie was shrieking and jumping around and Norelle was looking at me like I had two heads.

"You're *engaged*??" she marveled. "Or is this something you treated yourself with?"

"I treat myself with new computer equipment or fattening desserts. Not jewelry."

"Ohmygodohmy*god*!!" Dixie grabbed me and danced around in a circle, and I couldn't help but chuckle. It was nice that at least *one* of them was excited. "I'm so happy for you!"

Norelle was still looking dazed. "I didn't even know you *wanted* to get married, Lola."

I shrugged. "I never *didn't* want to; it just wasn't something I focused on. Certainly never thought about it with anybody before. But now..." I couldn't resist a smile as I looked down at the ring. "I've got the right one."

"Aww, cuz..." Dixie grinned, still holding onto my arm. "That's so beautiful! John is your soul mate! I sensed it the first time I met him."

"Yeah, he is."

"What do you call him?"

"John..."

"I mean, like, pet names."

"John..."

"Seriously, that's it? I call Ryan my Honey Boo."

"I don't think John wants me to call him that any more than I want to say it. The most I do is the occasional 'baby' or something OG like that. Though I admit that's usually during our special couple's workouts."

"Wow, you two go to the gym together, too? I didn't know that. The last time I saw you work out was when you were doing all that Tae-Bo."

Norelle rolled her eyes. "She's talking about *sex*, Dixie. Which must mean she's *really* sprung because that's the kind of tea she usually doesn't share."

"Guess I'm still high on the happiness fog." I winked at them as I moved around them towards the kitchen to get some juice. "Sometimes it has you acting outside of yourself."

"Uh-huh."

"So have you two set a date yet?" Dixie asked, trailing me. "Have you started planning? Where are you gonna do it? I can go with you to look for dresses. *Ooh*, Norelle, what are we gonna do for the bachelorette party??"

"I guess that's the bright side to all this, that I'll get to see some strippers," Norelle muttered, slinking into the living room and plopping onto the couch. "They'd better be super fine, though."

"I can ask one of the other bartenders at work; I know she just got married a few months ago and she was telling us about her bachelorette party. Y'all, she said there was one guy that danced for them that had the *biggest*-"

"Let's pump the brakes a little bit, okay?" I interjected, though I *was* curious to hear what colloquialism my clean-mouthed cousin would've used for 'penis'. "This isn't gonna be a big thing. Neither John or I want a big wedding."

"Oh. Well, that's okay. You can get married in a nice garden or something. Or maybe the park."

Knowing that's where John proposed made me smile. "Ehh. Really, we'd be fine just going to the courthouse."

"The *courthouse*??" Norelle exclaimed, sitting up. She was looking at me like I'd lost my mind. "Y'all have to do it up bigger than *that*."

"We don't care about a wedding. We just want to get married."

"You pregnant or something?"

"Why do I have to be pregnant?"

"Well, you're always at his house so I figure you two are doing plenty of *working out*. And this is *so* out of the blue..."

"We've been together for a year, Norelle. It's not out of the blue."

"Still, though-"

"It doesn't matter," Dixie interrupted, waving her hands. "Time doesn't matter when it comes to love. Ryan and I haven't been together as long as Lola and John and I know he's the one I want to marry."

"Getting married isn't everything," Norelle muttered, playing with the ends of her long black hair.

I looked at her curiously. I hadn't expected her to be over the moon about my news but I wasn't expecting her to be quite this sullen, either.

"What's up with you, Norelle?" I asked her, putting down the bottle of cran-grape juice in my hand. "Why are you so bothered right now?"

She and Dixie shared a look before there was a loud knock on the door, then it opened and Russell appeared. He looked at the three of us curiously, apparently sensing he'd walked in on something.

"What?" he asked.

"Oh, nothing," Norelle immediately replied, suddenly energetic as she sprung off the couch. "Just talking about Lola and John getting married."

"Ha! Yeah, right. That'll be the day," Russell scoffed, sweeping his long locs from his face. "As if Lola would ever marry anybody."

"She's engaged, you idiot."

"*What??*" His eyes snapped to me. He rushed over and grabbed my hand, gaping at my engagement ring. "He asked you to marry him, for real? And you said *yes*??"

"Why is this so amazing to you people?" I asked, removing my hand from Russell's grip. "I've made it more than clear how serious I am about John and that he was it for me, haven't I?"

"Yeah, but that's not the same as actually wanting to be locked with him *for life*," Norelle retorted. "You never once said you wanted to marry him."

"Yeah, well, I do. So I hope *my friends* can be happy about it with me. But it's happening either way, regardless."

"Of *course* we're happy for you, Lola!" Dixie insisted, still grinning. I could just imagine all the pink-tinted ideas whirling through her head about all the things we could do leading up to the big day. "We're gonna be right there with you through this whole thing."

"I appreciate that, cuz. Though I'm not sure there's gonna be a *whole thing*; I told you, we don't want a lot of fuss."

"Wait, if you're getting married, that means you'll be moving out," Norelle realized. "You're gonna leave Dixie hanging like that?"

"I'm not worried about that," Dixie immediately dismissed.

"You *should* be. You know you've never lived alone."

"Yeah, Lola, maybe you should reconsider," Russell added. "Remember, you made that promise to Dixie first. And she's your *cousin*. Family is supposed to be the *most* important thing, not our own selfish-"

"*Wow.*" I glared at him. "Did you just say *selfish*?"

"Okay, maybe that was the wrong word. But have you thought about what's gonna happen to Dixie in all this?"

"Actually, I have. And of course I was going to talk to her about all that. Let's stop acting like Dixie isn't a grown woman who can take care of herself."

"Yeah, guys, we'll work all that out," Dixie concurred with a wave of her hand. "I'm just so happy for Lola; that's all I'm thinking about. I'm right here to help you with whatever you need, Lola; just say the word."

I smiled at my cousin appreciatively. She could be rather...*young-minded* at times (hence the reason her mother asked me to let her move in with me; I've always been tasked with looking out for her, even when we were kids) but that didn't mean she was an idiot. And she always had my back, which I appreciated even more now that Norelle and Russell were acting like Downer A and Downer B.

"Thank you, Dixie," I replied pointedly, eyeing those other two. "At least *one* of you is good with all this."

"Well, I'm sorry for not immediately jumping for joy over you being so eager to marry some other dude before you ever gave me a *real* chance," Russell grunted.

"And there it is..."

"Damn, Russell, get *over* it, already," Norelle groaned. "You and Lola fooled around years ago and it's been over with for longer than that. It's a little sad that you're still harping on that, dude."

"Oh, yeah?" He glared at her. "Maybe *I* could say it's sad that you've been bitching around here for the past couple of weeks because Drone *dumped* you."

My jaw dropping slightly at this news, I looked at Norelle, who looked like she wanted to tackle Russell. "Dang...how come you didn't say anything, Norelle?"

"It's not exactly something I wanted to broadcast," she grudgingly replied, folding her arms in a huff. "It was kinda embarrassing."

"Yet Russell knows about it and I don't? And I'm guessing Dixie already knew, too."

"*They've* been here; *you* haven't," she retorted. "You're *always* with John. Plus, you're so in *love* and everything...I wasn't trying to tell you that I got thumped because I spilled juice on his Jordans. Who wants to admit they got dumped over some stupid mess like that?"

"Um, hello? Do you not remember Orlando kicking me to the curb for stepping on his game controller?" I reminded, referring to my ex. "I was right where you are fourteen months ago."

"And look at you now; engaged and moving on and everything." Norelle shook her head, snatching her purse from the couch. "I just remembered something I need to go do; I'll talk to y'all later."

"Seriously??"

"Norelle, come on..." Dixie pleaded.

"Actually, I should be out, too," Russell announced, giving me a parting frown before turning towards the door. "I have to...water my plants."

"Russell, you *know* you don't have plants."

"Later." The door slammed behind him.

Dixie just stood there in disbelief for a moment before turning remorseful eyes to me. I shook my head and took a long gulp of my juice, trying not to show how hurt I was. I didn't expect cheers and cartwheels (well, except maybe from Dixie), but the *last* thing I expected was for Norelle and Russell to get so upset to the point that they left. *Voluntarily*. That never happened.

"I'm sorry, Lola," Dixie said to me.

"Not your fault."

"They're just surprised by the news, is all. In a few hours, they'll probably be as happy for you as I am."

"Hmph. Can't say I'm holding my breath for that."

"You want me to make you some brownies?"

I couldn't help but smile. Dixie loved trying to comfort me with food. It was like offering a lollipop to a pouting toddler.

"Sure," I replied, realizing I actually wanted some brownies. She grinned at me. "No rush, though. I'm gonna go finish my laundry."

"Okay."

I went to my room and closed the door behind me, looking at the laundry basket on my bed but making no move for it. My mind was still processing my friends pitching a fit because I told them I was getting married.

Maybe I should've insisted on eloping and just bought John's mama a nice gravy boat or something.

TWO

"I didn't expect them to trip like *that*."

John slid my cupcakes over to me across the small table we were sharing at Pure Sugar, a local bakery. I'd just finished telling him about the drama from Norelle and Russell the previous day that, honestly, I was still marveling over.

"Me either, really." I peeled the wrapper off my PB&J cupcake, my mouth already watering a little bit. Peaches, the owner, was among the best of the best when it came to baking. "I expected a few snarky little comments to mess with me but I didn't think they'd actually get *upset*. I'm not gonna lie; I feel some kinda way about that."

"Totally understandable. Those *are* your best friends."

"Even if Russell was still a little jealous, I thought he'd gotten to where he accepted that I had moved on and was happy with you." I stuffed half the cupcake in my mouth, and John couldn't help but chuckle at me. I didn't try to be cute when I ate those things. "And I always thought Norelle was just joking when she'd make comments about how I was at your place so much. But I guess not."

"I'm sure they'll come around, though," John assured, unwrapping his own key lime cupcake. "I bet they'll be waiting on you the next time you go home, ready to do whatever you need them to."

"Well, I certainly haven't heard from them since yesterday. Not even a 'my bad, I was an asshole but I've got your back' text."

"Babe, you know they've got your back, though. Don't stress over it; this is supposed to be a happy time for us."

"True. At least my dad was on board when we told him this morning."

"I figured he would be. Your dad and I were cool from the jump. And I'm sure when we tell my folks later, they'll be just as happy about it."

"What time did they say to be there?"

"Four o'clock."

"Sure you don't wanna just go to the courthouse, get hitched, and then tell everybody later?"

He smirked at me. "It won't be that bad, babe."

"John, you know I've grown to love your family; well, except your sister..."

"Lola."

"What? It's not like she's a fan of mine, either. She's probably still hoping you get back with your slutty ex."

"We all know that's not gonna happen, though, so it doesn't matter."

"Yeah, well. I can't say I'm looking forward to dealing with her reaction, not to mention how jubilant your dad is gonna get, fracturing my ribs with his overly-aggressive hugs. It's like one extreme to the other."

"You're making this worse than it has to be; you know that, right?"

"I know you think I can be pessimistic. I'm just trying to prepare myself."

"Maybe try thinking positively? Just for the hell of it."

"Fine." I sighed, grabbing my cup of water as I sat back in my chair. "I'll...think happy thoughts or whatever."

"Thank you."

All this bubbly thinking only lasted so long, though, when we got to John's parents' house and found more than just John's parents there.

"I didn't know y'all were gonna be over here," John commented once he saw his brothers Jude and Jimmy once we entered the den.

"Jessa's on her way, too," Jimmy informed, casually flipping through a magazine.

"Excuse me?"

"When you said you had something to tell us, I figured everybody should be here," John Sr., John's father, loudly explained as he entered the den behind us, patting John on the back so hard that he stumbled forward a little bit. He was one of those people that didn't mean any harm but tended not to recognize his own strength. "So I told them to come by."

"That really wasn't necessary, Dad. This wasn't supposed to be a family meeting."

"Well, it is one now, since I put off my game for this," Jude grumbled, arms folded. He looked like he didn't want to be there, which I strangely appreciated.

Jimmy chuckled. "Man, just un-pause the video game when you get back."

"Shut up, Jimmy."

"Hello, Lola," Marilyn, John's mother, greeted in her silky-smooth voice when she entered the den carrying a couple of large bowls of chips. No surprise that she was the first one to directly address me since we arrived. "It's so good to see you. You're looking beautiful, as usual."

"Thanks so much, Ms. Marilyn."

"And when are you going to stop with all this *Ms.* stuff and just call me Marilyn?"

"I'm working up to it," I admitted, returning her smile. "I appreciate you letting us come over."

"Please, you two are always welcome here."

"So what is this about, son?" John Sr. asked, taking one of the bowls of chips (that was surely meant to be shared by everyone) and putting it in his lap as he took a seat in his recliner.

"Oh, well, I just wanted to-"

"Aren't you gonna wait for Jessa to get here?" Jude asked, cutting him off. "You're just gonna have to say whatever it is all over again."

"Uh, no, because Jessa is always late and I'm not trying to wait on her," John replied firmly. "And like I said, I didn't call all of y'all, anyway."

"Look, if you two are gonna have a baby, you could've just let us all know that in the group chat."

"We're not...shut up, Jude. Mama," John sensibly focused on her, since she was the most level-headed, besides maybe

Jimmy. "What I wanted to tell you was that Lola and I are getting married."

"You what??"

Of *course* Jessa would walk in right when he said that. If only I'd known about that group chat sooner...

"That's wonderful!" Marilyn exclaimed, coming over to give John and I hugs. "I'm so happy to hear this!"

"Yeah, I figured it was only a matter of time, as sprung as you are," Jimmy teased his little brother, slapping hands with John. "Congratulations, bro."

"Thanks, man."

"*I'm getting another daughter-in-law*??" John Sr. bellowed, reaching over and slapping John on the back. Marilyn managed to grab the bowl in his lap before he shot out of the chair, snatching me up into one of his bear hugs. "Welcome to the family, sweetheart!"

"Thank you; I'm excited about it," I managed to say, though he was squeezing me like a stress ball. I couldn't help but grin, though, since at least he was happy about the news. He'd welcomed me ever since we first met. I patted his shoulders as he lowered me back to the ground.

"You sure you wanna marry this one here?" Jude asked with a smirk, nodding his head towards John as Marilyn gently took my left hand to peruse my engagement ring. "He's not exactly loads of fun, you know."

"I love him just the way he is," I insisted, grinning at my fiancé. He winked at me.

"You two are seriously getting married?" Jessa finally spoke up, apparently snapping out of her trance. "You've only been together for, like, a minute."

John rolled his eyes. "It's been a year, Jessa."

"Really? Already?"

"Yes. Already."

"When is the big day?" Jimmy asked.

"We don't know yet."

"Of course we've gotta have an engagement party," John Sr. announced. Loudly. "We can have it here at the house!"

"We'll need to let everybody know, so more people can be here," Jude added. "I'll bring the booze."

"I'll DJ," Jimmy offered.

"Whoa, whoa, everybody chill for a second," John (thankfully) spoke up, holding up his arms. Because I was starting to itch at all this impromptu party planning. "Thanks for wanting to do all that, but we don't need an engagement party. We just want to get married and that's it; we're not trying to have a bunch of extra stuff."

"Oh, come on, you've gotta celebrate this good news at least a little," Jude insisted. "You mean to tell me you don't want one last night of ignorance before you tie the knot?"

"That's what I'm telling you, Jude. When have you known me to enjoy *nights of ignorance*?"

"See what I mean?" Jude shook his head. "No damn fun at all. How are we even brothers?"

"Believe me, you're not the only one to wonder that."

"Getting married is a big deal," Jessa needlessly informed us. "Are you two sure you're ready for all that? Or are you just hopped up on pheromones?"

"Jessa; hush and sit down," Marilyn ordered, frowning slightly. Another example of why she was my favorite. "If you can't say something positive, just be quiet."

"Thanks, Mama," John said as Jessa stomped over to the loveseat and dropped onto it in a huff. "We just wanted to let you know 'cause you're family, but really, Lola and I could just go handle it at the courthouse tomorrow and be done with it."

"The courthouse?? We won't hear of it!" John Sr. immediately retorted. "You two *have* to have a real wedding!"

"We don't want a lot of fuss, Dad."

"Fuss? This is your *wedding*!"

"I know, but we-"

"Is this a shotgun wedding? Usually when people want to rush to the altar, it's 'cause there's a baby on the way," Jessa inserted.

"I am *not* pregnant," I spoke up. Oh, how I wished we had done this all this on speakerphone.

"We understand that you want to keep things low-key," Marilyn spoke up, giving a pointed look to her husband and offspring. She turned her eyes back to me and John. "And this is *your* wedding, so you should have what you want."

John and I both sighed in relief. "Thanks, Mama."

"It *would* be nice, though, if you would let us celebrate this with you in *some* small way, though," Marilyn continued. "It doesn't have to be a big event. Maybe a barbecue or a just something informal here, where you control the guest list. It can just be the people in this room and whoever Lola would like to include."

Gosh, these people were persistent.

"We don't want to stress you out. It's just that John is my baby boy..."

Sighing, John looked over at me, silently asking my permission to relent. Part of me wanted to stick to our plan but the bigger part knew I couldn't deny his mother what she was asking. It was a reasonable request.

I gave John a slight nod and he squeezed my hand before turning back to his mother. "All right, we're good with that. As long as it's *just* like you said..."

"I promise," Marilyn insisted. "I won't try to sneak any more people in here."

"We can bring our wives, though, right?" Jude asked, regarding him and Jimmy.

John hesitated. "Yeah, I guess."

"Well, if they're bringing their dates, I'm bringing one, too," Jessa proclaimed.

"They're bringing their *spouses*. You don't have one of those."

"I can still bring a date."

"It's not necessary to bring a date to this, Jessa. We don't want a bunch of people here. So either come alone or stay home."

"Damn, it's like *that*?" She looked at me like I was the one who told her that instead of John. Though I agreed with him a hundred percent. It wouldn't have bothered me at all if she stayed her negative behind at home.

"Yeah, it's like that," John replied, his voice strong. "I'm telling you straight-up what the deal is now so you don't try to pull something like you pulled at Thanksgiving."

"I didn't *pull* anything. I told you, I only invited Chandra because she said she was gonna be alone for the holiday."

"I don't care. You knew I was bringing Lola to meet the family and you bring my ex in here? Then you two spend the whole time making your stupid slick comments to my woman? Don't try to act like you didn't know what you were doing."

"I said I was sorry for all that. I don't even talk to Chandra like that anymore."

"Only because you found out she cheated on me when we were together. And I don't recall you apologizing to *Lola* for how you acted."

He and Jessa stared each other down before Jessa sighed and looked at me. Her short locs had grown out some since I last saw her. I'd probably think she was really pretty if her attitude hadn't clouded my judgment.

"Sorry."

This was her idea of an apology? How moving.

"Thanks," I replied, with equal unenthusiasm.

"Well," John Sr. shouted, clapping his hands together. If it were anyone else I'd think he was just trying to break the tension, but he was just naturally loud. "That settles that. You two let us know when you're ready to have this party-"

"*Not* a party," John corrected.

"Gathering, then. And we'll make it happen."

"Fine."

John and I left a little while later. He dropped me off at home since he had some running around to do, and I just wanted to decompress from that whole visit. And I was looking forward to having the place to myself, since I knew Dixie was going to be out, and Norelle and Russell were still in their feelings. I still hadn't heard from them at all.

Turns out I didn't have to wait long, though, because when I opened the door to my apartment, I saw them both. And let's just say his feelings weren't the only thing Russell was *in*.

They were so into what they were doing that they didn't even notice me standing there with my jaw on the ground.

"What the *hell*?!"

"Lola!"

"Shit!"

They scrambled to get up, trying to keep themselves covered. Thankfully they were under one of my blankets, which I was going to have to now burn. But at least I didn't see anyone's bare ass.

Norelle wrapped the blanket around her while Russell awkwardly buttoned his pants, standing apart from each other. As if it wasn't too late for that. Neither of them would look at me.

"You're back," Norelle finally muttered, tucking some hair behind her ear.

Smooth. "I'm trying to decide what I'm more shocked about...the fact that you two are having sex, or the fact that you chose *my apartment* to do it in."

"We didn't think you'd be home."

"The place where my name is on the lease and I pay bills and live and where all my stuff is? Imagine that."

"Dixie said you were gonna be out with John."

"You have your own apartment, Norelle," I reminded her. "In this same damn building. *Why* are y'all...since *when* did y'all-"

"It just happened, all right?" Russell finally spoke up, still looking away. "We were here with Dixie earlier, then she left."

"We stayed here 'cause there's something wrong with the heat in my apartment," Norelle explained.

I quirked a brow. "That shouldn't have been a problem, given what you two were doing."

"Lola. Look, we were talking about how things went down yesterday, and admitted that it was kinda messed up how we reacted. We got to talking about that and a bunch of other stuff, then we had some alcohol delivered. After a couple of bottles of wine, one thing just kinda led to another."

"We've all gotten drunk together before and not *once* has it led to sex."

"I was upset about Drone, Russell was upset about you. We were just making each other feel better. He kissed me-"

"Uh, no...*you* kissed *me*," Russell corrected, looking at her.

"No...*you* started it, Russell."

"No, I didn't, Norelle."

"Yes, you *did*! Remember? I dropped my phone, we both went to pick it up, then you ended up on top of me..."

"What??"

"You know what? I don't need the details," I insisted, holding up my hands. "I'm already gonna have a hard enough time trying to get the image of the two of you sexing on my couch out of my head."

"If it makes you feel any better, we're both cool with you getting married now," Norelle said, as if that was supposed to make me feel better right then.

"Great," I deadpanned. "I feel...*so* much better now, knowing that. Thanks."

"I know that's sarcasm, but this isn't anything bad, Lola," Russell insisted. "If anything, you should be glad about it. Less drama for you."

I gaped at him for a moment before pressing my fingers to my temples. My head was suddenly throbbing something serious.

"I need to lie down," I droned, eyes closed. "And since I don't wanna be wondering if the two of you are in here knocking boots against the refrigerator, I need you both to go."

"Wait, are you upset?" Norelle asked me. "Are you mad at us for this?"

"What you two do is your business; you're both grown. I didn't love *seeing* it, but whatever. My problem is you *doing* it on my furniture. Not to mention, it taking you so long to realize how messed up your reactions were yesterday."

"Lola..."

"Y'all, I've had a rather draining day, as it was, and this just didn't help any."

"We're sorry about that..."

"Look, whatever. I just don't wanna be bothered right now so if the two of you can please just clean up this all these bottles and stuff and leave, I'd really appreciate it."

Not waiting for a response, I just went to my room and closed the door. I couldn't *believe* I had actually seen my two friends getting it in live and in person. There was no *way* I would have ever guessed that Norelle and Russell would have ended up together, even if it was just a fling.

Shuddering at the memory, I popped a couple of Tylenol, took off my shoes and jacket, and stretched out on my stomach on the bed, pulling a pillow of my face to block out the light from the window. For the time being, I didn't want to deal with anything or anyone else.

All I knew was whoever said the thing about how being engaged was supposed to be one of the happiest times of your life was mistaken.

THREE

I had told myself to think positively about this engagement shindig. It wouldn't be so bad, I figured; a few hours with some friends and family celebrating me and John about to start our lives together, and all that. Easy peasy, right?

Yeah, no. I was already over it.

First off, what was supposed to be a gathering of about ten people, aside from me and John, turned into about twice that.

Jessa's hardheaded ass brought a date, even though John told her not to. Which of course caused a big argument between the siblings that Marilyn had to diffuse.

And thanks to John Sr. apparently running his mouth, other family members showed up, supposedly 'totally by coincidence.'

Dixie was uncharacteristically late, and when Ryan dropped her off, somehow he and Jude got to talking and then Jude invited *him* to join us.

And Norelle and Russell arrived together, which I wouldn't have thought anything of any other time, except I still (unfortunately) remembered what I caught them doing on my couch.

Jimmy turned on some music, then Jude decided to blast it, which only made everyone have to talk louder to be heard over it.

There was no alcohol in the house. And I wasn't even a huge drinker but I surely wanted it then.

So, needless to say, I wasn't in the best of spirits. As much as I tried to put on a happy face and ignore the nonsense, I was supremely annoyed. I hated that John and I (mostly John) agreed to this engagement party thing, because I should've known it was going to turn into something we didn't want.

"What's wrong?" Dixie asked me, finding me where I was loitering in the kitchen cramming pretzels.

"I want to leave."

"Leave? This is *your* party!"

"Doesn't feel like it. This is *not* what we wanted."

"I know how you get around groups and a lot of noise and commotion. But everyone is here to celebrate you and John getting married."

"Are they? 'Cause I can't tell that. Nobody has even acknowledged that that's what this whole shindig is about; it might as well be just any other family gathering."

"Okay, but we all know it's not. Can't you just try to have a good time?"

"I tried, Dixie, but I'm over it. I only agreed to this to appease John's mother. And they clearly didn't respect our wishes so excuse me if I'm not walking on air."

"I get it; I just wish you wouldn't be so bummed. You've been in a mood this whole time and it's evident."

"That's why I'm in here instead of out there. Not trying to be a buzzkill. And I don't wanna keep seeing Norelle and Russell put on their little act."

"What act?"

I remembered Dixie still didn't know about our friends' little tryst. Even if we weren't at my supposed engagement party, I wouldn't have told her; she'd just freak out and I'd have the task of calming her down.

No, thanks. I'd let them tell her about their...whatever they were doing...on their own.

"Never mind. Forget I said that."

"I'll go get John," Dixie suggested, placing a brief hand to my shoulder. "Maybe he can get you to cheer up."

I just shrugged, wondering if John had even noticed I was missing from the action.

Dixie scurried out, and a few minutes later, John was standing in front of me.

"What's up, babe?" he asked, looking concerned.

"Nothing," I shrugged again. "Dixie wanted you to come in here."

"Why? I was wondering where you'd gone. What's wrong?"

"I'm annoyed, John," I admitted, putting down the pretzel I'd been nibbling on and turning to him. "This whole thing...this isn't what we talked about."

"Yeah, I know it's a little more than what we discussed..."

"You're being nice."

"I'm making the best of it. It already started off on some bullshit with Jessa; I wasn't trying to let that ruin the whole day."

"Well, that's good for *you*, but I'm having a harder time enjoying all of this."

"Maybe that's because you're not even trying."

My eyebrows shot up. "What?"

"Lola, I get it; my family overstepped with this. But not in a *terrible* way; all they did was invite more people to celebrate us getting married. I could see if they were opposing it but everyone is thrilled for us, babe."

"Jessa isn't."

"Jessa is *one* person. I'm not basing everything on her. Why do you always have to find the downside of things?"

"I'm not trying to be negative for the sake of it, John."

"I've been watching you; you've barely smiled all day. I have a feeling that even if everything was exactly like Mama promised, you'd still be unhappy about *something*. Be honest; you just don't wanna be here."

"Wow..." I took a step back from him, actually a little hurt by his words. "That's what you think?"

"Am I lying? Don't think I don't notice how standoffish you are around my family, Lola. Ever since you met them at Thanksgiving, you've kept them at arm's length, being all detached and not making any *real* effort to get to know them better. You tolerate them because you have to, not because you want to. And I've kept my mouth shut because I hoped you'd come around in your own time. But I'm starting to wonder if you even want to do that."

The way he was looking at me set off a strange feeling. "What are you saying?"

"Do you *really* want this, Lola?" He looked right into my eyes. "Do you really want to be my wife? Because, as much as I love it, it's not gonna always be just me and you in our own space; my family comes with the deal. Yeah, they can be a lot, but you know they mean well. Is this how you're gonna be around them, or anyone else you're not in the mood for, indefinitely?"

Flashbacks to a little over a year earlier came to my head, when my ex Orlando and I were having a similar argument. My introversion was a big issue with him, and part of the reason he dumped me right before Christmas. He might have blamed it on me stepping on his controller, but we both knew what the real deal was.

That breakup didn't affect me, though, because I didn't want to ultimately end up with Orlando, anyway. But if John ended things...there'd be no getting over it any time soon.

"John..."

"Hey, I was wondering where you two had snuck off to."

I hadn't even heard Marilyn come in; John and I were just standing there looking at each other.

Marilyn's smile faded slightly as she noted the clear tension in the room. She looked back and forth between us with concern. "Is everything all right?"

"Not really," John replied before I could give her an automatic pacifying answer. His eyes were still on me. "Unfortunately."

"I don't want to pry, but..." Marilyn stepped closer to us, standing between our face-off. "Is there anything I can do?"

"No, Mama. Thanks, but this is something Lola and I have to work out ourselves."

"Understood." Marilyn set the empty pitcher she'd been holding on the counter and turned to leave. Before she did, though, she looked back at us. "John Sr. and I fought the night before our wedding, and I called everything off. That was almost forty years ago. All I'm saying is...remember why you wanted to marry each other in the first place."

She left, and John and I continued to look at each other. Her words gave me a teeny bit of hope but I couldn't tell if John had even heard her. I wondered if he was regretting proposing to me, even a little bit. But I admit I didn't the nerve to ask.

"You were saying?" he urged once we were alone again.

I'd actually forgotten whatever it was I was going to say when Marilyn interrupted us. But another thought replaced whatever it was.

"Are you really that frustrated with me? How I am; does it bother you that much?"

His eyes roamed my face before he stepped forward, taking my hand. I felt a hope surge. "There's always going to be things that we don't like about each other. I've known how you are for a while, babe, and I still proposed. So clearly it's not a deal-breaker."

The tightness in my chest eased a little.

"I love you just the way you are, Lola. And I know you love me the way I am. But we *both* have room to improve. And I hope that now that I've pointed this out to you, you'll be mindful of it. I just want everyone to get along the best we can."

"I get it."

"Do you, really?"

"Yeah, John. It's automatic for me to want to retreat into my own shell at times but I never mean to be rude to anyone. I do hope you know that."

"I'm sure you're not, babe. But I can't say that's not how other people see it. You just give off this vibe at times that you can't be bothered."

"Not the first time I've heard that."

"So?"

"So...I'll try to do better. I don't want to be at odds with your family or anyone else."

"Good."

He was leaning in to kiss me when we heard a commotion in the den. We both rushed out to see Norelle and Russell looking sheepish and disheveled just outside of the guest bathroom, a few surrounding people talking to or about them, and Dixie looking like she was about to faint. Her papersack brown skin was about as pink as the blouse she was wearing, which I might've laughed at any other time.

"Umm, is this what it looks like?" John muttered in my ear from behind.

"It's exactly what it looks like."

"I didn't know they were together like that."

"I don't know *what* they're doing. At least now I'm not the only one that apparently caught them in the act."

"This is turning into a mess."

"Your words."

"Where's your dad?"

"Probably outside taking a smoke. I get my commotion-aversion from him."

We just stood there for a moment and watched Norelle and Russell stammer an explanation for why they were banging in the bathroom, and Dixie screech question after question about what this meant and if they were a couple or not, and other people either denouncing their nerve or praising them for it. Maybe this would've been entertaining for some people but it was just making my head hurt.

The scene was just starting to disperse when we heard Jessa and her date arguing loudly in the den, which of course, everyone flocked to.

I didn't even try to comprehend what they were fighting about and neither did John. He moved past me to stand in between them, his arms outstretched.

"I don't know what this is about, but can you two either take it outside or save it for later?" he asked them, clearly agitated. "This is supposed to be about me and Lola, not all of you all's drama."

"Well *he* shouldn't have said what he just said!" Jessa argued, pointing at her date.

"Ooh, what did he say??" one of John's sisters-in-law asked (I admit I was still a little fuzzy on their names and oftentimes got them mixed up).

"Doesn't matter!" John exclaimed before Jessa could answer. "This is *exactly* the kind of mess we were trying to avoid. Can y'all not respect what we're supposed to be here for?"

"Come on, man, don't get so stressed," Jimmy chimed in. "We're all family."

"So what? That means I'm not supposed to say anything when y'all act crazy?"

"At least you and Lola will be able to say you had an interesting engagement party, son," John Sr. suggested, actually grinning like we'd agree with that. "There's always a bright side!"

"That is not a *bright* side, Dad."

Just then, Jude turned up the music, apparently trying to drown out the arguing. John looked helplessly at Marilyn, who could only shrug apologetically. Even she knew when she was beat.

Over it, I just went to get my purse. Nobody really even noticed as I headed right out the front door, thankful that I'd had the presence of mind to drive my own car.

I was sure John would get miffed at me for leaving without a word. I'd just have to cross that bridge when I got to it.

"Where you goin'?"

Dad was sitting in his car, windows down, seat reclined, listening to Al Green while smoking a cigarette. He blew smoke through his slightly darkened lips as I headed over to him, his dark eyes eying me.

"I've reached my limit," I told him, standing a little ways back to avoid his smoke. "It's just too much."

"Where's your man?"

"Still in there, trying to diffuse things."

"He knows you're leaving?"

"I might not have mentioned it to him..."

"Think that's smart?" He took another drag. "You can at least let him know."

"I'll text him. I don't wanna go back in there."

"So you gon' run every time the family gets together? Not sure how that's gonna work, Lola."

"I'm not gonna do that. Just doing it today."

"Mmm-hmm." He tossed his cigarette to the ground, and I instinctively ground it out with my shoe. He grabbed a soda from his passenger's seat and I wondered how long he'd been out there. "Just don't forget, the family comes with the man. You're gonna have to learn how to deal with it."

"Dad, you're sitting out here in your car."

"This party wasn't for me; *I'm* not marrying anybody. And I'm just saying, how's it gonna look for you to skip out on your own engagement party without a word?"

I knew he had a point. But even though my head was telling me I should go back inside, it also replayed how things had gone since the whole 'engagement party' started. And my desire to go back in didn't budge.

"John will understand," I replied, hoping it was true. "Love you, Dad."

"Love you, too."

I headed to my car, got in, and drove home, hoping that my friends didn't show up any time soon. I knew John had probably figured out I was gone by then, and I knew he wouldn't be happy about me dipping out. Now that I'd had time to cool off, I questioned my decision to leave without telling him. Might not have been the smartest thing I've done.

Before I could call him, though, he was banging on my door.

"What the hell, Lola?" he demanded as soon as I opened the door. He looked good and angry. "You just leave and don't even tell me?"

"I'm sorry; I realize now I shouldn't have done that..."

"You realize it *now*. You didn't see anything wrong with it *then*?"

"At the time, John, all I cared about what getting away from all of that mess." I took a seat on the couch, rubbing my hands along my thighs. "Even after you called them out, it didn't make any difference. And I just got fed up."

"And you couldn't let me know that?"

"I...I don't have a defense for that. I should have. Guess I figured you'd understand."

"You thought I would understand my fiancée leaving my parents' house in the middle of our engagement party without telling me? You really thought I'd be cool with that?"

"I didn't say you'd be cool with it; just that you'd understand it. Come on, John, that was not an engagement party and you know it."

"Regardless of what it was, Lola, we were supposed to be there *together*." He stood there glaring at me, arms folded. "And we had *just* talked about how you act around my family. Do you know how embarrassing it was when I was looking around for you and realized you had left? I should've found that out from *you*, not your dad."

"John, I...I admit that was something I didn't consider. I'm sorry about that."

He just shook his head at me for a moment before sucking his teeth and turning away.

"Can you sit down?" I requested.

"No, Lola, I don't want to sit down."

"Okay, I get I could have handled things better today. But we need to talk about it."

"Oh, *now* you wanna talk? The talking should have happened *before* you snuck out and left me hanging." He headed for the door.

"John!" I shot off the couch. "Are you seriously leaving?"

"Yeah. I'm seriously leaving."

"You're not..." I didn't want to say the words but I had to know. "You're not breaking things off with me, are you?"

He was already out the door.

FOUR

"Lola?"

I rolled over on my bed, turning my back to the door. Company was the last thing I wanted. Hopefully Dixie would get the hint and leave me alone.

"Lola."

That was Russell. No sense in wasting energy asking what he was doing there.

"Can you please answer the door?" Norelle. "We were worried when no one could find you at the party. What's going on?"

Knowing they weren't going away, I rolled off the bed and trudged to the door. They all gasped when I opened it, looking at me with some kind of shock/horror mix.

Dixie actually pointed at my face. "Have you..."

"Yes, I've been crying. I *am* capable of that, you know. I'm not a robot."

"But you hardly cry. Last time I saw you in tears was after your mom passed."

"And that was years ago," Russell added.

Sighing, I wiped my face with both hands before stuffing them under my arms. "What do y'all want?"

"We're just checking on you. What happened? You've been locked in here ever since we got back," Norelle observed. "We thought you'd be with John."

"Did you two have a fight or something?" Dixie asked as I turned back towards my bed, my energy to stand there gone.

And of course, they all followed me. "It must be something pretty major to have you in here crying like this."

"We're just trying to make sure you're okay," Russell added.

"Why do *you* care? You and Norelle didn't have anything but complaints when I told y'all about my engagement. Really, you haven't been very supportive of my relationship with John at *all*, Russell, so I'm not sure why you're in here acting concerned now."

He sighed. "Lola…look, I'm sorry about that. But I'm good with you and John now. He's a good dude."

"Why? Since you're banging Norelle, you don't have to worry about what I'm doing anymore?"

They gasped, as if they couldn't believe I'd say such a thing. Good. Hope I offended them.

(Well, except Dixie. *She* didn't act stupid when I announced my engagement).

"Lola, come on," Norelle pleaded, perching herself on the edge of my bed. "Don't be like that. We know we could've handled that better than we did. I know *I* felt bad about the stuff I said once I had some time to think about it. You were happy and we should've had your back. We're sorry."

"I see you're speaking for the both of you. So you two are a couple now?"

Norelle and Russell exchanged a glance. "We're just…exploring. There's no title yet."

"Hmph. Well, I'll have my insensitive remarks on the ready for when you come in here talking 'bout you're in love and engaged. Then you'll see how it feels."

"Lola."

"We're nowhere *near* all that," Russell insisted. "Look, I get that you're pissed at us, but can we make it up to you? How 'bout we all go out to celebrate your engagement. It's on me."

Squeezing my eyes shut, I shook my head. "That might not be necessary."

"What do you mean?" Dixie hurried over to sit next to me on the bed, placing a hand on my back. "Did you and John have a fight? Is that why you left the party?"

"No." I sighed, sitting up and wiping my eyes. "We had a fight *because* I left the party."

"What happened? Why *did* you leave?"

"I wasn't feeling the party at all, as you know, Dixie. John came in there and checked me because of my *attitude*, saying I was being standoffish and that I seemed to only tolerate his family rather than really getting to know them. And I admit he had a point. I was going to try to put all the other stuff out of my mind and just make the best of it, but then you two horndogs got caught in the bathroom and Jessa and her date got to arguing, and John's family seemed to be dismissing his concerns, and I just couldn't stand it anymore. So I left."

"You didn't tell John you were leaving?"

"No. I know I should have, but I didn't. He followed me here, let me have it, and walked out. Wouldn't stay and talk about it or anything."

"Oh, Lola..." Dixie slid an arm around me. "I'm so sorry."

"Is that why you're crying?" Norelle asked. "Because y'all had a fight?"

"Fights happen. I'm crying because it seemed like that might've been our *last* fight. I asked him if he was ending it between us and he didn't even answer me; he just left."

"Girl...he's probably just pissed off. I doubt he'd end your relationship over this."

"That was a couple of hours ago and he hasn't called or texted," I sadly noted, looking at my phone for the hundredth time since John had left earlier. "We've had our disagreements but it's *never* been like this."

"Lola, I'm willing to bet he's just getting his head together," Russell offered. "If he *really* wanted to end it, he would have."

That gave me a mild sense of hope. When I asked John if he was ending it, he didn't say *no*; he just didn't answer at all. Maybe that meant he just needed some time.

"I hope you're right," I sighed, making myself put my phone down. I rested my head on Dixie's shoulder. "Because I sure don't want that."

"If you want my advice, I say you should go over there," Norelle suggested, gently nudging my leg. "Don't let this sit and give him time to stew over all this; he might talk himself into thinking things are worse between you than they are. Go over there and get your man; work this out."

"Before you do that, though, make sure you're ready to *really* deal with what the problem is," Russell spoke up. "Don't just seduce him into not being mad at you without being willing to really change anything. 'Cause if you two do get married, this *will* come up again. All I'm saying is, make sure you're taking his concerns as seriously as you want him to take yours."

He was right. I had to check myself. That whole scene at Thanksgiving had tainted my mind towards John's family, and that wasn't fair. Really, everyone had been really nice to me, except for Jessa. She was the only one I had a real problem with.

"Thanks for that, Russell," I said with a small smile. "I definitely need to have my stuff together before I go over there."

It was another couple of hours before I gathered the nerve to finally call John and ask if I could come over. When he agreed, I took a super quick shower, threw on some sweats, and headed over, telling myself to think positively.

"Thanks for letting me come by," I greeted once he opened the door.

"Why didn't you use your key?"

"Didn't think I should."

He just looked at me for a moment before stepping aside. "Come on in."

I couldn't remember the last time I'd been so nervous. When he closed the door and we settled in the living room, there was a tiny part of me that wondered if it would be the last time...

"You sure you wanna do this?"

I looked over at John. "Are *you*?"

"Absolutely." He brought my hand to his lips and kissed it before leaning down and kissing my lips. "Never been more sure of anything."

It was almost midnight, and John and I were in the wedding chapel in our sweats and sneakers, waiting our turn to get married.

We'd had a long talk. A *really* long talk. Not just about what happened at the engagement party; about everything; things we had been holding our tongues about, what we expected from each other in our relationship and marriage, compromises and adjustments we each needed to make. We didn't agree on everything and at times the conversation got a little testy, but we both stayed and worked through it because there with each other was where we wanted to be.

And at the end of it, we decided to just forget everything else and do what *we* wanted. And what we wanted was to get married and start our lives together. No fuss, no muss.

So, marriage license in hand, we went off to a late-night wedding chapel. And honestly, I'd never been happier.

"I, Lola, take thee John – the *best* thing to ever happen to me—to be my lawfully wedded husband," I recited, grinning at my man as we held hands in front of the chaplain.

"I, John, take thee Lola – my intelligent, sexy, beautifully introverted Lola—to be my lawfully wedded wife," John stated when it was his turn, returning my grin and giving my hands a little squeeze. His eyes were glistening a little bit.

We exchanged rings before finally being pronounced man and wife, and John immediately pulled me to him, kissing me like we were alone in the room. Our arms wrapped tightly around each other as we admittedly got lost in the moment, to the point where the chaplain had to clear his throat a couple of times to get us to come up for air.

"It's me and you now," John whispered, resting his forehead against mine.

I nodded, still grinning. It probably wouldn't be going anywhere any time soon. "That's how I like it."

A while later we were sitting at a back table at Toast and Butter, pigging out on stacks of sweet cream pancakes with blueberry syrup. There were only a couple other people in the restaurant, and when the owner Ridge learned that this was our post-wedding meal, he gave us extra flapjacks on the house.

"How mad do you think everybody is gonna be when they find out?" I asked, reaching for more syrup. It was made fresh there every day and good enough to drink through a straw.

John shrugged as he finished chewing the bite he'd just stuffed into his mouth. "They'll probably be pretty ticked off. But I'm sure they'll get over it, especially once they understand our reasoning."

"And once we tell them we're willing to have a big reception and invite everybody, maybe that'll speed up the forgiveness train."

"Probably. Even Dad had acknowledged that things got crazy at the engagement party so I'm sure they'll understand. Either way, we're already married." He reached over and took my hand, smiling. "Nothing they can do about that."

"Not a damn thing."

Bonus story:
Goodbye, Introvert

ONE

I had just gotten into my car when I got a call from my husband. Even after six months, it still felt weird to say that.

Smiling, I answered the call. "Hey there."

"Babe," my husband John greeted, making me smile wider. I admit I was still high off the newlywed fog. "Where are you?"

"About to head over to Norelle's."

"Yeah? Y'all just gonna hang out?"

"She said she had some news. Knowing Norelle, there's no telling what it is."

"It's just gonna be you or are Dixie and Russell gonna be there, too?"

"I'm sure they will be. You know the three of them are practically joined at the hip. This must be something special, too, since we're meeting up at Norelle's. I was actually starting to wonder if she even still *had* an apartment, since she was at my and Dixie's place so much."

John chuckled. "Well, maybe her place is the spot since you moved out."

"I guess. She's been acting kind of strange lately, though. I think she said she was coming down with something; probably caught it from one of the kids in her class."

"That sucks. Dixie is still cool with living alone?"

"Oh yeah, she's fine. She's with her man Ryan half the time, anyway. But you know I'm still getting the occasional comments about me having the nerve to get married and change the group dynamic. They act like I'm not right across town."

"Yeah. Well, things change. I'm sure they'll get used to it." John's voice sounded different all of a sudden, but I brushed it off. Probably just my imagination.

"True. Did anything interesting happen at work today?"

"Uhh...I guess it depends on what you consider interesting," John replied. "I'll tell you about it when you get home."

His voice still sounded off to me. "You okay?"

"Yeah." His response was quick. "Yeah, I'm fine, babe. Just a long day. Can't wait to see you."

"Now, see, don't be tempting me to make up an excuse and stay home."

He laughed. "I know that's your natural inclination but nah, don't do that. Go hang with your friends; y'all need that time together. I'll be here when you get back."

"Okay." I still felt like something was up with him but I wasn't going to press it. John was one of the most level-headed people I knew; if he said he was fine, I'd leave it at that. I knew if it was something major, he'd tell me. "I'll try not to be too long. Can't wait to see you, either."

"I love to hear it. What do you want to eat?"

"We can just get some pizzas while we watch the game. And fool around, of course."

"Of course. That's a bet, then. Let me know when you're heading back."

"I will. Love you."

"Love you, too."

I headed on over to the apartment building I'd recently moved from, automatically starting to head to my old apartment before I caught myself and went to Norelle's. I couldn't help but be curious as to what this meetup was about; Norelle wasn't usually one for grand announcements. Maybe she had finally hit on one of those lottery scratchoffs she was always buying.

Dixie and Russell were already there when I arrived. They looked surprised when I came in.

"What?" I asked.

"I was kinda wondering if you'd show up," Norelle commented from where she was sitting crisscross applesauce on the couch. She looked tired, with her long black hair pulled into a messy ponytail and her dark skin makeup-free. She didn't even have her false lashes on, and she wore those things religiously.

"I thought we agreed the little digs about my not being around here as much were going to stop." I nudged her knee as I picked up one of the couch pillows and plopped down into the corner. "Didn't we?"

"I just meant that you were really busy with work, since you got that new project."

"Oh." I looked at Norelle, who didn't seem like her usual spunky self. "You all right?"

"We've been asking her that since we got here," Russell informed from his spot in the mismatched armchair. "She didn't even clown Dixie for that Powerpuff Girls shirt she has on."

"Okay, now I'm freaked out..."

"Speaking of shirts, Lola, how come you're not wearing the one I got you after you eloped with John?" Dixie asked me. "I had that specially made."

"Dixie...cuz...as much as I adore bright pink bedazzled hoodies with 'Hot Bride' on the back, it's not really something I can wear out and about without feeling ridiculous. But if it makes you feel any better, I *do* rock it around the house."

"Good. As long as you didn't just throw it in a box or something and forget about it."

"I wouldn't do that. It's actually pretty comfortable; I like to put it on when John is being kinda stingy with the thermostat."

"*Isn't* it comfortable?? I got one made for myself, too. The back says 'Hot Bride's Cousin.'"

"So, Norelle, now that we're all here, can you tell us what this is about?" Russell requested. I guess he didn't enjoy the girlie hoodie talk. "You've barely said anything since we got here."

"Yeah, you don't seem like yourself," Dixie added. "What's going on?"

Norelle chewed on her lip for a few moments before taking a deep breath and flopping against the back of the couch. "Drone called. He wants to get back together."

Russell's head jutted forward. "That's it? *That's* what you told us to 'get our asses over here' for?"

"I thought you never wanted to hear from him again after y'all broke up," Dixie commented.

Which I didn't blame her for. The guy dumped her because she accidentally spilled juice on his sneakers.

"I didn't," Norelle concurred. "I told him to go to hell and hung up on him."

"Okay..."

"But part of the reason I did that was because..." Norelle took another deep breath. "I'm pregnant."

"You're *what?!*" Russell, Dixie, and I all screamed, jumping out of our seats. Norelle didn't flinch; she just sat there looking at the floor. She'd barely made eye contact with any of us since I got there.

"Are you for real??" Russell exclaimed.

"Come on, Norelle, this isn't funny," Dixie chimed in. "Are you just messing with us?"

"You're seriously pregnant?" That was me. "You said you weren't gonna have kids until they invented a way for you to hatch them."

"Yeah, well, looks like I'm not gonna be able to wait for that scientific breakthrough. In about seven months, I'm gonna be somebody's mama."

"Seven months? You're already two months in and you're just now telling us?"

"I wasn't sure myself 'til I finally went to the doctor. I thought I was feeling like crap all of a sudden 'cause one of my students gave me their little nasty germs. But nope."

"Oh my god, Norelle," Dixie marveled, her hands mashed against her chest. "Are you...happy about it?"

Norelle just shrugged a shoulder and ran her pinky nail around the elastic cuff of her sweats.

I guess I had to be the one to ask. "So if you're pregnant, who's the father?"

Norelle's eyes turned to me before sliding over to Russell, who had gone momentarily mute. He was sitting stiff like he was trying to recreate the statue at the Lincoln Memorial.

My jaw dropped and so did Dixie's. We both slowly turned to Russell.

A few moments passed before he said anything. Finally, he cleared his throat and spoke, though his eyes were still on the floor in front of him. "It's mine?"

Norelle nodded, eyes still on him. "Yep. It's yours."

"And you thought this would be the best way to tell me?"

"What's the difference? Might as well tell all of y'all at the same time."

"Uhh, *no*...I think I deserve to be told in private instead of you springing it on me the same damn time you tell everybody else."

"I tried a couple of times to tell you when we were alone, Russell, but I punked out. It was just easier on me to do it this way."

"Easier on *you*?"

"Y'all, come on," I jumped in before they got too riled up. Or rather, before Russell did, because buddy looked like he wanted to leap out of his chair. "Let's focus on what's important. We know now; let's just deal with it."

"How are you feeling, Norelle?" Dixie asked her, placing a hand on her shoulder. "Are you okay?"

"No, I'm not okay. I'm freaked out!" Norelle exclaimed, making Dixie jump. I'd probably have laughed at that any other time. "This was *not* supposed to happen! I'm not ready to have kids! Do you know how long it's been since I changed a diaper? Do you know how much diapers *cost*?? I haven't even gotten my car paid off yet!"

Okay *that*, I couldn't help but chuckle at. Norelle glared at me.

"Norelle, girl, I know this is a big deal, but try to calm down," I told her, the smile still on my lips. "You're just in shock right now."

"Yeah, you'll figure it out," Dixie assured her. "And we're right here to help you."

"I thought you said you were on the pill," Russell piped up, as if he'd just remembered that. He sat forward in his seat. "When we ran out of condoms and you said we didn't need any? So that time we went raw-"

"Y'all can save this part of the discussion for when Dixie and I aren't here," I insisted, cutting him off. I didn't need to hear that. I'd already seen them in action when I caught them sexing on my couch one time; that was more than enough detail for me.

And Dixie apparently agreed since she literally had her hands over her ears.

"Did you lie to me?" Russell demanded to know, scowling at Norelle. "Did you try to get me to knock you up on purpose??"

Norelle scoffed. "Do I *look* like someone who wanted to get knocked up on purpose? And why would I try that, anyway? You a Zamunda heir or something?"

"But you *did* lie, though, right?" Russell persisted, ignoring her sarcasm. "About being on the pill?"

"Russell..."

"Guys, let's not do this," Dixie pleaded, holding up her hands as she looked back and forth between them. "Arguing isn't going to do anyone any good, plus Norelle, you don't need to get any more stressed out than you already are. Think about the baby."

"The baby." Russell ran his hands down his face. I'd never seen him so anguished. "So I guess you're keeping it?"

Norelle cut her eyes at him. "Yes, I'm keeping it."

"Don't act like that's a stupid question. You were the one just screaming and hollering about how you're not ready for kids."

"Well, I'd better *get* ready, 'cause it's happening."

"You mean we. *We'd* better get ready. It's my baby, too."

"Oh, trust me, I know. I'm not gonna forget whose hardheaded sperm did this to me."

The laugh escaped before I could stop it, and Norelle and Russell frowned at me. Dixie tried to look admonishing, though I could still see the glint of amusement in her eyes, too.

"I'm glad you think this is funny," Russell grumbled at me, crossing his arms in a huff.

"I'm sorry, but y'all aren't exactly making it easy to keep a straight face." I tried to tamp my smile down some as I pushed my locs off my shoulder. "You two can't be at each other's throats right now, is all I'm saying. You've been fooling around for a while now and you got careless. It happens. What's done is done. Pointing fingers isn't going to help anything."

"Are you two a couple now?" Dixie asked them. "Or are you still insisting you're not *together*-together?"

Norelle and Russell shared a look before looking away. "Hell, I don't know," Norelle muttered. "I'm still hoping I'm going to wake up any second now."

"Girl, the sooner you accept this for what it is, the better off you'll be," I told her. I grabbed hold of her forearm, waiting for her to look at me. When she finally did, I continued. "Don't stress, okay? For real. We've got your back."

"Yeah, we do," Dixie agreed. She grabbed Norelle's other arm. "This is a blessing. You two are gonna have the cutest little chocolate baby. It's gonna be so awesome. I can't *wait* to babysit!"

Norelle's lips quirked with a smile. "Y'all heard it! You're my witnesses! I hope you remember that when I'm calling you to come watch my screaming child so I can take a nap."

"*Or* you could just call me," Russell spoke up. There was no more frown on his face. "I'm gonna be right there with you, Norelle. We'll figure this out."

Norelle looked at him, her expression softening. "I know."

Russell stood, brushing his own long black locs over his shoulder before reaching for Norelle's hand and pulling her up. He wrapped her up in a hug, and Dixie and I grinned at each other.

"Is this gonna be you next, Lola?" she asked me. "You're the married one around here."

"Oh no," I quickly shook my head. "It'll be a while before John and I do any procreating. No, we're good just like we are right now."

I might've spoken too soon on that.

TWO

It was a couple of hours before I got back home. John was in the spare bedroom that we both shared as an office when we worked at home, which was most of the time. He came out to greet me when he heard me come in.

"Hey, babe." He pulled me to him, granting me those lips I couldn't get enough of. He was so freaking cute. "I was wondering how long you were gonna be. Is everything cool with Norelle?"

"Ehh...I guess that depends on how you look at it."

"I don't get it."

"She's pregnant. By Russell. And they're not exactly over the moon about it."

"For real?" John marveled, stepping back. "So I guess that answers the question of whether they're still messing around or not."

"Oh, they are. Or at least they have been. They've just been trying to keep it low key, for whatever reason. It's not like we all didn't already know about it."

"Guess they had their reasons."

"Hmm. Well, regardless, there's a baby on the way. Norelle was freaking out and Russell wasn't pulling out any cigars but they were feeling a little better about it by the time I left."

"That's good. It doesn't have to be a bad thing."

"Not at all. It'll be cool to have a little crumbsnatcher around. And Dixie and I assured them that we'll be right here to help with whatever."

John's easygoing expression tightened, and he stepped back even further. "Right. Umm...you hungry? I ordered the pizza already when you said you were on the way. It should be here in a little bit."

"Yeah, I am kinda hungry." I eyed him as he suddenly became way too interested in folding the throw blanket I'd left on the couch last night. Which wouldn't have been strange at all if it hadn't already been folded when he grabbed it. "What's up with you?"

He smoothed nonexistent wrinkles from the blanket. "Hmm? What do you mean?"

"John. Please don't act like I don't know you. You've got something on your mind; what is it?"

He finally looked at me and sighed. Grabbing my hand, he led me around the couch and sat, eying me as I followed suit. Nervousness pinged through my body as to what this might be about. He was acting strange and it was throwing me off.

"There *is* something on my mind," he concurred, his hand still gripping mine. "And I'm not sure how you're gonna feel about it."

"Is it bad?"

"I guess that depends on how you look at it."

"Are you throwing my words back at me to lighten the mood or because it actually applies?"

"It actually applies."

"Okay, you're freaking me out...just tell me."

"All right." He inched closer to me. "My boss called me in to a meeting today with a bunch of the higher-ups in the company. Long story short, they offered me an I.T. management position. Big raise, more perks, all that."

I gasped, then threw my arms around his neck. "Babe, that's awesome! I'm so proud of you!"

"I appreciate it." He hugged me back, though I couldn't help but note he wasn't as excited as I was. When I pulled back, he seemed as anguished as Russell had earlier when Norelle sprung the baby news on him.

"What's wrong? Why don't you seem happy about this? It's what you wanted, right?"

"Most definitely. I'm thrilled about the position; what I'm worried about are the terms. Well, one of them."

"Which one?"

"We'd have to move, Lola," he finally admitted, looking at the ground before turning his creamed coffee-colored eyes back to me. "The position is in Brodence."

"Oh..." I hadn't been expecting that. I kinda felt like the wind had been knocked out of me. "But Brodence is only a couple of hours from here and you telecommute most of the time, anyway. You *have* to move?"

"Apparently so, yeah. And believe me, I asked. I'll still be able to telecommute some but I'd need to be around there more, since I'd be in charge. If I want the position, I don't have a choice."

"Wow." I rubbed my hands along my thighs, processing all this.

"I told them I had to talk to you first before I let them know one way or the other, which they understood. They know we just got married a few months ago. They'd cover all the moving expenses."

"Generous."

"Babe, I know this is a big deal," he said, placing a hand over one of my sliding ones. "This is where you grew up. Your dad is here, your friends are here. Not to mention your own job, which you love. It's a lot to ask you to leave all that."

"Yeah, but...John, you can't pass up this opportunity. There's no way I'd ask you to do that."

"This affects *both* of us, Lola. It's not just about me."

"*Your* family is here, too," I reminded him.

"Yeah, but all I have to do is tell them how much my raise is and they'll probably come pack our shit themselves."

I busted out laughing at that. He was probably right, knowing his family as I did. His mama would be proud of him but wouldn't want him to go; he was her baby boy, after all. Everyone else would be trying to get him to Brodence on the next thing smoking. In the most supportive way possible, of course.

John was smiling at me, waiting for me to calm my giggling self down. "How 'bout we just pause and think about this, okay? They're giving me a few days to decide; we don't have to rush into it right now."

I was just about to respond when the doorbell rang. John got up to go get our pizza and I sat there replaying our conversation.

Moving?

I guess this was the day for big news.

We ate our pizza and tried to focus on the baseball game on TV, but my mind wasn't really on it and I'm sure John's wasn't either. Even when he tackled me on the couch and got me all hot and bothered before I pulled him to our bedroom so we'd have more room to finish what he started, I'm sure it was still in the back of our minds. Yeah, Brodence might've only been a couple of hours away, but this was still a big deal.

After John rolled from on top of me two fun, sweaty rounds later, I laid on his bare chest while he held me tightly, neither of us saying anything. My fingers trailed back and forth across his stomach while his grazed up and down my arm.

"Hey," I finally whispered.

"Yeah."

"Let them know tomorrow you're taking the job."

I didn't look up, but I knew he was looking down at me. "I thought we were gonna wait to discuss this."

"There's no reason to wait, John. Do you want this promotion?"

"Yeah. *Hell* yeah. But-"

"No, then that's all I need to hear." I sat up and looked at him, resting my chin on my arm that was laid across his chest. My eyes roamed his ridiculously adorable face. "It's a change but I can deal with it. And it's just in Brodence; we're not moving across the country or somewhere overseas. It'll be fine. *I'm* fine."

"Lola, are you *sure*?" he stressed, his hand squeezing my shoulder. "I don't want you to feel any pressure."

"I'm your wife, John; where you go, I go. We're in this together. And I'm damn sure not gonna stand in the way of you taking an opportunity you've worked years for. I love you. And I *want* this for you. Seriously; it'll be all right."

Blowing out a relieved breath, he rolled me onto my back, grabbed my face and kissed me hard and deep. I can imagine that he'd been stressing about this ever since he got the job offer. One thing I loved about him was that he always considered me and how I'd feel about things before he made a decision, even if it was to his inconvenience. But he didn't have to worry about anything; I was all in.

"I love you *so* damn much, Lola," he whispered, wrapping me up in his arms and burying his face in the crook of my neck. "You have no idea."

My eyes burned with appreciative tears as I held him as tight as he was holding me. I wasn't usually terribly sentimental John had a way of turning me into pure mush. And his feelings were definitely not one-sided.

"I love you, too," I whispered back, sniffling. Tears were actually streaming down my face but I didn't try to stop or hide it. "More than I've ever loved anything or anyone."

And I did. John was everything to me.

Yes, leaving my dad and my friends would suck and I was sure I'd have my moments when I missed their crazy asses, but that's what phone calls and Facetime were for. This was a good thing.

Now I just had to convince them of that.

Not wanting to put this off, I invited my friends over a couple of days later, telling them I got a new deep fryer and I wanted to break it in. Can't go wrong with the promise of free food, especially with Russell.

At least he and Norelle were in better spirits. Neither of them had the attitudes from when Norelle broke the pregnancy news. Thankfully they'd started putting their energy towards getting themselves right for their budding baby than arguing about how it got made.

Dixie was especially giddy, but no one really thought anything of it; my cousin got hyped over making a good batch of muffins or finding more stuff in pink. There was no telling what had her bouncing off the walls now.

"Is John here?" Norelle asked, kicking her shoes off.

"Yeah, he's in the back."

"I forgot there were so many of them," Russell mumbled, looking at a framed picture of John's family on the mantle. Aside from John's parents, John Sr. and Marilyn, he had two older brothers, Jimmy and Jude, and a younger sister, Jessa. That was the heffah I didn't like; I was cool with everybody else. Russell looked over at me. "Are they pressuring y'all to have kids yet?"

"Not really. They've joked about it to mess with us but they know we're not ready for that yet."

"That doesn't necessarily mean anything," Norelle muttered. "Look at *my* pregnant ass."

"Part of me wondered if that's why you invited us over here," Dixie chimed in, dancing over to look at the pictures with Russell.

I shook my head as I plunked the freshly-fried cheeseburger eggrolls into a pan lined with paper towels. "I'm not pregnant."

Though that would've been easier to tell them than what I really *did* call them over there for.

"That smells so good, Lola," Dixie complimented, coming over to the kitchen. John's house – *our* house – was open concept, so I could talk to my friends while they chilled in the living room. Hopefully our new house in Brodence would have the same thing because it had spoiled me. "You need any help?"

"I appreciate it, cuz, but I'm almost done. Just one more batch of hushpuppies."

"You must still be riding high from getting married or something, 'cause you don't usually host like this," Russell observed, taking a seat next to Norelle. "You used to try to think of ways to get us *out* of your spot but now you're actually inviting us over *and* feeding us?"

"Hey, no complaints here," Norelle made sure to say.

A few minutes later, we were all piling our plates with the delicious fried goodies. I made sure to set some aside for John before my friends gobbled up everything. He had agreed to stay in the office so I could tell everyone about the move on my own; I didn't put it past Russell and/or Norelle to turn their ire on John if he was sitting right in front of them. Though it took a whole lot of convincing to get John to agree to that.

While we stuffed our faces, I wondered how I was going to come out with my news. Then Dixie suddenly screamed and scared us out of our damn minds.

"What the hell??" Russell exclaimed.

"What is wrong with you??!" Norelle demanded, a hand on her heaving chest.

"I'm sorry but I couldn't hold it in anymore!" Dixie was literally shaking in her seat; I half expected her to shoot off the couch.

John came in to see what all the commotion was about, but I gave him a wave to let him know everything was fine. We weren't fighting; my cousin was just nuts.

"I'm engaged!" Dixie practically screamed, taking her engagement ring out of her pocket and jamming it on her finger before waving her hand around. Norelle had to catch it mid-air so we could look at it. "Ryan proposed last night!"

"Congratulations!" I put my plate down so I could hug her, which she gleefully accepted. I pulled back and got a closer look at the ring. Ryan surely had good taste. The teardrop pink diamond was perfect for Dixie. "I'm so happy for you, cuz."

"Thanks, Lola!"

"I guess we don't have to ask what your answer was," Russell teased, making us all laugh. "Good for you. Ryan's cool."

"He certainly is. Hey, maybe you and Norelle will-"

"Nope!" Both Russell and Norelle cut that off immediately. I chuckled.

"Let's just worry about us having this baby together without me having to pull all his locs out," Norelle suggested, stuffing half a chicken tender into her mouth.

Russell rolled his eyes. "Or me having to super glue her mouth shut."

"Lola, I want you to be my matron of honor," Dixie announced, turning to me. "Will you?"

Damn it.

If I wasn't moving anywhere, there would've been no hesitation. I'd gladly do that for Dixie, not just because she was family but because she was always there for me. When I got engaged to John, she was super supportive while Norelle and Russell copped major attitudes about it. They eventually apologized but that didn't mean I forgot how they acted.

Being matron of honor meant having to help with everything, and that wouldn't be as easy to do from two hours away. Not impossible, but I knew my cousin; she'd want me to be right by her side, physically, through all this. Because I already knew she wanted a big wedding; eloping like John and I did wasn't even an option.

I figured this was as good an opening as any to tell them the real reason for this fried food shindig.

"You know I'm more than happy to do that for you," I began, actually feeling a little nervous. "But there is something you should know first."

Dixie frowned curiously. "What do you mean?"

I didn't have to look at Norelle and Russell to know they were eying me, too. Might as well just spit it out.

"I'm moving."

There was a long pause, and I wasn't sure if it was because they didn't hear me or because they thought I was joking.

"You what?" Norelle asked.

"I'm moving," I repeated a little louder. "John and I...we're moving to Brodence."

Dixie's jaw dropped, apparently snapping out of the temporary trance. "What?? Wh-you're *moving*? Why??"

"You *just* got married and moved in here," Russell needlessly reminded me. "What, you didn't like this house and couldn't find another one in the same city that you wanted instead?"

Lord. "Not even close, Russell."

"So what are you moving for, then?"

"Because John got a great promotion that he can't pass up. That I won't *let* him pass up," I made sure to add, before they started shifting any blame to my husband. "It's too good of an opportunity for him."

"For him? What about *you*?" Norelle asked, putting her plate down. "What about *your* job?"

"I'm a web designer; I can do that from anywhere. Brodence is just a couple of hours away; I can still work from there and come back here for any super important stuff."

"Wow." She folded her arms, sitting against the back of the couch in a huff. Russell just blew out a long breath and stared down at his food.

"You're really leaving?" Dixie asked, her voice wavering. Tears were already threatening to fall. "I can't believe it."

"Come on, y'all, don't do this..." I pleaded. I almost wished they tripped out like they (namely Norelle and Russell) did when I announced my engagement. That was way easier to deal with; it pissed me off, easy-peasy. But this, with them getting so sad and emotional and teary, this was unfamiliar territory. It made me a little uncomfortable, actually.

But I knew I had to deal with it. These were my closest friends; I couldn't just tell them to get over it and go back to eating their hush puppies.

"I need you here, Lola," Dixie said, a tear running down her cheek. "I'm about to get married; I'm excited but I'm scared.

And it's always been me and you, since we were kids. I don't wanna do this without you here."

"Dixie...cuz, I'm still gonna be here," I assured her, taking her hand. She used her other hand to wipe her face with her sleeve. "We can talk on the phone, Facetime...and you know I'll come here for the big stuff like your dress fitting or the rehearsal dinner or whatever y'all wedding-happy people do. Things will be a little different but I still have your back; nothing's changing about that."

"What about *me*?" Norelle spoke up. "I'm about to have a baby; I was gonna ask you to be the godmother."

"I can still be the godmother."

"But what about when my hormones start going all over the place; I was counting on you to be here to keep me in check. We all know I'm gonna freak out when I start gaining weight and my boobs get all big and start leaking milk. And pregnant women fart a lot; did you know that?? There goes being sexy. I *like* being sexy! And do you know how much baby stuff costs? My nose is gonna spread...even my *feet* might get bigger! I read about that in the baby book. Thanks a lot for giving me that, *Russell*!"

"O-kay..." I tried my best to keep my face even because I really wanted to laugh at her crazy ass. "I think we can check the hormones part off the list. As for the rest of it, everybody's pregnancies are different, from what I hear; I doubt you'll get every single thing they mention in the book."

"But what if it *do*?" she whined. "Russell isn't gonna know what to do and Dixie will probably just freak out right along with me. Especially since she's gonna be in bridezilla mode. You keep all of us right, Lola."

Wow. I guess I hadn't realized just how big a part I played in their lives. It was touching. And flattering.

"Norelle, that is really sweet. And a little bit of pressure. But mostly sweet. And again, I'm still gonna be around; you can always call me when you need to vent or fuss or whatever."

"Remember you said that 'cause I'm damn sure gonna hold you to it."

"I don't doubt it."

Russell was looking at me. I couldn't quite read the look on his face.

"What's up, Russell?" I asked cautiously. Part of me wondered if he was going to start tripping about John taking me away from them or me breaking up the group.

It took a few moments but he finally spoke. "I don't want you to go, Lola. But..." He looked down at his hands rubbing together. "I get it. You've gotta be with your husband. And John is a good dude, and I know he's good for you. I've never seen you as happy as you've been since you got with him. So you've gotta do you."

I blinked, surprised. "Thank you for that, Russell."

"Yep." His eyes were still on his hands. Dixie was still crying and sniffling and Norelle was pushing her chicken fingers around on her plate.

"But can y'all please stop looking so sad? Please?" I pleaded. "I'm not leaving the country. Y'all are still my people. I'm gonna be here for all of this that's going on...Russell and Norelle having your baby, and you getting married, Dixie. And y'all can come visit us; Brodence has some cool restaurants. I read about one place that's supposed to be just as good as Toast and Butter."

"Hush your mouth," Norelle pointed at me, unable to resist a smile. I knew that would get at least one of 'em. "Toast and Butter is the shit and nothing in *Brodence* can touch it."

"I guess we'll see, won't we?" I grinned at her, then looked at Dixie and Russell. They tried to fight it, but pretty soon they were finally smiling back at me. I breathed a sigh of relief; I wasn't great in heavy situations and I just wanted them to feel better about everything. It would've sucked if they were so bummed or angry about my leaving that they held a grudge about it.

Dixie threw her arms around my shoulders, resting her head against mine. "I really am happy for you and John, Lola."

My smile grew as I took hold of her arm that was across my chest. "I appreciate it."

"And don't forget what you said about me calling you," Norelle reminded me. "I'm gonna do it."

"Oh, I know."

"If John starts acting up, make sure you call me," Russell ordered. "You know I'll handle that."

"I know, Russell." I nudged his knee. "But I don't think you'll have to worry about that. Like you said, John is a good dude. He's been nothing but good to me."

"He'd better be."

"When are y'all leaving?" Dixie asked.

"In the next two or three months; they're helping us find a place in Brodence, and of course we have to get everything wrapped up here."

"Well, I guess we'll just have to soak up every ounce of Lola time we have left." Dixie started squeezing me like a big stuffed animal, throwing in some shakes for good measure.

"Right..."

Russell picked his plate back up. "You want us to throw y'all a going away party?"

"Of course not."

"We're gonna do it anyway."

"Of course you are."

"Why hasn't John come out here?" Norelle asked.

"He had some conference calls. Plus, I didn't want y'all ganging up on him."

"We wouldn't do that."

"Yes, you would."

"Okay, we would. But it's all out of love."

"Sure."

We fell back into our regular rapport of messing with each other, and their appetites apparently returned because all the food except what I had set aside for John was gone by the time they left. But at least no one was crying anymore. Hopefully that would still be the case when moving day came.

THREE

Time seemed to speed by once I told my friends about me and John moving. We had told John's family a couple of days later and they reacted just as John said they would; not thrilled about him leaving, but proud of him for being awarded such an opportunity. His mother Marilyn was more emotional about it than any of them, which we also expected. But she assured us she was happy for us both. So was my dad.

It didn't take as long as I thought for us to find a house we both loved in Brodence. It was an adorable brick bungalow with four bedrooms, two baths, and the open concept that I wanted. It even had a nice little backyard, which would be good for whenever we were ready to start popping babies out.

Finding a house made the concept of moving a lot more real, and I had to make myself not freak out about it. As much as I was on board with John making this career move and doing what he needed to do for that, there *was* a small part of me that was bummed about leaving my family and friends. I didn't know anyone in Brodence and I wasn't exactly a pro at meeting new people and making friends. I liked the friends I had.

But I kept that to myself, though, because I didn't want John to feel bad. He was already asking me every other day if I was okay and wondering if I'd had second thoughts. And he had enough to worry about, with the new position and all the added responsibility that was going to come with it; I wasn't going to add any more stress. At the end of the day, I knew it would be all right.

I should've known Russell wasn't kidding about throwing us a going away party. John and I were still in the process of getting everything packed up and I honestly didn't have the energy for all that, but Russell did not care.

"I don't wanna hear it," he wasted no time telling me when I tried to tell him that. "Y'all are leaving in two weeks and before we know it, you'll be gone. So I suggest you get some coffee or some Red Bull or something and get your asses over here."

"All right, all right." I should've known he wasn't gonna let me off the hook.

Between packing, getting things together for the move, and work, the day of the party snuck up on me. John actually had to remind me; I was about to lay down for a nap.

"You know we need to leave in about an hour, right?" he said, amused, as I was burying myself under the comforter on our bed.

"What?" I poked my head out, my locs falling over my face. "Leave for what?"

"The party at Russell's?"

"Dammit..."

"How do I remember that and you don't?"

"I think I thought it was *next* weekend."

"Nope. Tonight."

"Wonderful." I let my head fall back onto the pillow briefly before making myself throw the cover off me and sit up. "I should've tried harder to talk him out of this."

"I know you're tired," John said, offering his hand to help pull me off the bed. "We both are. I'm not exactly in the mood for a party, either, but I appreciate them wanting to give us a send-off. And really, things are gonna get so hectic in the next couple of days or so that it's pretty much now or never."

"True." I gave him a quick peck on the lips before trudging towards the bathroom. "Guess I'd better start getting ready, then."

"Do you know who all's gonna be there?"

"Hopefully just Russell, Norelle, Dixie, and probably her fiancé Ryan. Maybe Dad, if they can get him out of the house. Russell didn't mention anyone else."

"Well, hopefully it's not a repeat of our engagement party where everybody and their mama showed up."

"Ugh. Don't remind me."

I didn't love thinking about that day not only because John's family completely ignored our request to keep things low key, but because John and I had a huge fight thanks to me getting irritated and leaving the party without telling him. For a moment, I sincerely thought he was going to break up with me over that but thankfully, we worked it out and eloped later that night. Just the two of us.

We both got showered and changed, then headed over to Russell's. It had been a while since I'd been at his house, since he was always at my or Norelle's place. I had to think that he just didn't want us messing up his stuff because his spot was a little nicer than ours, really.

"I was wondering if you were going to try to make up an excuse to get out of coming," he said as soon as John and I walked through the door. "I was prepared to come get you myself, if need be."

"Not necessary. We're here."

"I'm gonna need you to perk up, though," he requested, kissing my cheek and bumping fists with John. "You look like you're already ready to leave."

"I'm tired, Russell. I've got a lot going on with work, and moving is a pain in the ass."

"I empathize. Still, though. I actually bought groceries for this."

"Well, aren't you just the Black male Martha Stewart."

Norelle and Dixie were in the living room, and they rushed over to us as soon as we entered, practically knocking me and John over.

"I was wondering if you were gonna actually show up," Norelle stated, still gripping me in a tight hug.

"Why does everyone keep saying that?"

"Norelle, see, I told you they wouldn't flake on us," Dixie insisted. "You owe me five dollars."

I glared at Norelle while John chuckled. "You bet on this?"

"Maybe." She actually tried to look innocent.

"You better be glad you're pregnant."

"Is anyone else coming?" John asked Russell, who was bringing in bottles of wine from the kitchen.

"Yep. They should be here any-"

The doorbell ringing cut him off and he went to the foyer to answer it. Norelle was slumped on the couch, eying the wine bottles longingly.

"I won't be able to enjoy you for another five months," she sighed, rubbing her baby bump.

"That's so sweet, talking to your little nugget already," Dixie grinned. "They say that's good for the baby, to hear that."

I shook my head. "Dixie, cuz, she was talking to the wine."

"Oh..."

John and Ryan chuckled as people started filing into the living room. John's parents, followed by his brothers, sisters-in-law, and Jessa. I told myself to be nice to the heffah as they all came over to give us hugs. A couple of minutes later, my dad arrived.

"What did Russell say to get you out of the house?" I teased as we shared our usual one-armed hug.

"He said I could smoke my cigars in the house."

"That'll do it."

"Plus I figured I might not get to see ya before you left if I didn't."

"Aww, Dad. We would've definitely come by to see you before we left."

"Uh-huh."

"There's appetizers in the kitchen," Norelle announced to everyone. "Dixie made 'em 'cause I wasn't about to do all that."

"I'll bring them in," Dixie offered, hopping up from the couch. She grabbed Ryan's arm. "Come on, sweetie."

"Y'all can put your jackets and stuff in our room, if you want," Russell called out. "It's the last one down the hall."

It took a second for his words to register and when they did, my head whipped around to Norelle. "Wait a minute...*our* room? Last I heard, Russell lived alone."

Norelle looked a tiny bit sheepish. "Oh yeah, guess we forgot to tell you about that..."

"Uh, *yeah*. You two are shacking up?"

"As of last weekend."

"I thought you two weren't *together*-together. Now you're moving into his house?"

"Lola, girl, this is more about practicality than romance. My lease was up. And Russell was calling me every other hour asking how I was doing, driving me nuts. It just made more sense to move in here so we'd be in the same space and can deal with all the baby stuff together."

"So this is only about the baby, huh?" I eyed her skeptically. "You're trying to tell me you and Russell haven't done *anything* since you moved in here? You're apparently sharing a room."

"Well, hell. We might as well, since I'm here. These hormones have me horny all the freakin' time. And I'm already pregnant. It's not like he can double-stuff it."

I cracked up at that. Part of me hated that I wouldn't be nearby to see firsthand the two of them trying to cohabitate. I could only imagine the arguments they'd had already.

Everyone milled around, talking and laughing and noshing and drinking. We all naturally broke off into little groups; I was huddled up with Norelle and Dixie; John, Ryan, and Russell were cutting up with John's brothers, Jude and Jimmy; John's parent's were with Dad and Jessa. I knew Dad really wanted to smoke but was refraining due to Norelle being pregnant.

After a little while, Russell called for everyone's attention. I could only hope he didn't ask me to give a speech or anything.

"Thank y'all for coming," he began. "I figure we'd better get the show on the road before these two introverts start giving me the eye or find some excuse to slip out."

Everyone laughed, though he wasn't wrong. I'd been resisting the urge to look at my watch for what had to be a good half hour.

"We just wanted to give you all a nice send-off to let you know how much we love you and are gonna miss you and all that," Russell continued. "And because we know y'all, we kept it to just the people that are closest to you. And don't worry; I'm not gonna ask either of you to say anything."

"Thank you," John and I chorused, his arm draped around my shoulders.

"But if anybody *else* has a word for the departing newlyweds, here's your chance."

"I'll go first," Dixie immediately spoke up. I could already see the tears glistening in her eyes and could only hope she managed to keep it together. "Lola, you've been looking out for me since we were kids, and I'm still trying to get used to the idea of you not being nearby anymore. But thankfully, you won't be too far away. And I'm *so* happy for you and John; you two were made for each other. I just hope my honey Ryan and I are as happy as you two are. I love you."

I grinned at her as Norelle chimed in. "You already know how I feel about you, girl. We've been down since college and I'm closer to you than I am my own rachet sisters. I don't even like them heffas but I love *you.*"

We all laughed, but she wasn't kidding at all and I knew it.

"John, I hope you're not gonna have a problem with me blowing your wife's phone up 'cause I'm still gonna need her support while I go through the rest of this pregnancy, and *especially* after I give birth. And y'all *better* come back here to visit!"

"Of course we will," I assured her. "You being somebody's mama is not something I wanna miss."

"Shut up."

"I'll go next!" John Sr. called out, as usual totally unaware of how loud he was. "John, I'm proud of you, son. You're movin' on up and you have a beautiful wife beside you while you do it. Be sure to call your mama at least once a week so she won't worry herself to death. Her hair is already half gray."

Marilyn nudged him playfully. "Hush. Though I *do* hope you two will stay in touch. It's going to be an adjustment, one of my babies not being nearby anymore. But I am so very happy for you two."

Next up was Jimmy. "I'm happy for the two of y'all, too. I never thought that John would meet a woman that was as much of an introvert as he is but he met his match."

Jude: "I'm still tripping that my little brother is going to be making more than I am. I need to step my game up. But I'm proud that me and my brothers all found dope Black women to marry and hold us down. Too bad Jessa is still by herself."

"Shut up, Jude," Jessa grunted. Her frown eased as she turned her eyes to John and me. "But for real, John, I'm not thrilled about you leaving but I understand you've gotta do what you've gotta do. And Lola, I know we're not exactly BFFs but I see how happy you've made John, and I can't be mad at that. I really do wish the two of you the best."

Then to my complete and utter surprise, my dad stepped forward. "You were barely a teenager when your mama passed, and it's been just me and you ever since. You're a good daughter; you see about me but you don't hound me. And I've always said that if you ended up with anybody, that it was with a man that appreciated and loved you for who you are. You've got that in John. And I know already know he's gonna take care of my baby girl."

"Absolutely, sir," John assured, giving him a gracious nod. The grin was still on my face as I blew my dad an appreciative kiss.

After my two sister-in-laws (whose names I always got mixed up) said a few words, John stepped forward, his hand gripping mine. "Thank you all so much for this. I'm sure I can speak for my wife when I say that we really do appreciate all of you for the support. It would take a hell of a reason for us to leave y'all so it's good to know you have our backs as we start this new chapter. But thankfully, Brodence isn't too far so I don't want anyone to be thinking of this as a *goodbye*."

"Oh no, 'cause we're still gonna bother you," Norelle insisted. "You already know, Lola."

"Oh, I do, believe me," I chuckled. "I couldn't get rid of you if I wanted to."

"Nope."

"Well, I'm sure nobody expected this but I'm gonna say something, too," I made myself say, playfully rolling my eyes at the dramatic gasps that erupted around the room. "Don't worry, it won't take long. I just wanted to say how much I appreciate all this. We both do. I know I'm not huge on crowds and gatherings but it's different when it's family. And y'all mean a lot to the both of us."

I raised my glass and everyone followed suit. To my surprise, I actually felt myself getting a little choked up.

We all hung out for a while longer, the evening turning into a semi-roast with people telling random stories about me and John from the past, and a couple of people surprised us with going-away gifts, which we hadn't expected. By the time we finally left, I was emotionally spent, but feeling warm and tingly from all the love. Even Jessa had given me a hug before we left.

"That was nice, huh?" John asked when we were heading back home.

"It was." I smiled at him. "You see I actually made a mini speech."

"Yeah, I know. I thought Russell had slipped something in your wine."

"Maybe he did. I even stopped checking my watch after a while."

"Still no second thoughts?" He glanced over at me before turning his eyes back to the road.

"No, John; I told you I was good. Though I *will* admit that this is all getting so real now that it's so close. I've never lived anywhere else, other than when I was in college."

"It's a big step. But I'm grateful they're just moving us to Brodence and not somewhere way off. And I'm not gonna front like I'm not nervous about the promotion, too; it's a lot of responsibility."

"You can handle it. This is what you've been working towards. Pretty soon they'll be offering you *another* promotion."

"I love that you believe in me so much."

"Of course I do."

"When we get home, I'm gonna show you how much I appreciate that."

I looked at him as my body flared up in anticipation. "I'm gonna need you to drive faster, then."

Moving day came before I was really ready for it. I was exhausted from all the packing and the preparing, not to mention still working during all this. Thankfully I was still able to keep my job where it was, since I worked from home ninety percent of the time, anyway. So that was one thing among many that wasn't changing.

Dixie, Norelle, and Russell insisted on coming by to see us off, which I both loved and hated. Loved it for obvious reasons, but hated it because I knew Dixie would get super-emotional, and I didn't have the energy for that. I'd been hoping I'd endured all of the going away sappiness at the actual going away party.

"I know I've said it a hundred times, but I still can't believe you're actually leaving," Dixie said, sniffling. "Everything is changing all at once."

"Yeah, pretty soon *none* of us will be in our old apartment building, after you move in with Ryan," I replied, stashing my purse in the front seat of John's car. I glanced at the moving trucks stuffed with me and John's things. "It's kinda wild to think about."

"I'm sayin'. We had a bunch of good times there," Norelle added, chomping on a breadstick, of all things. That was her latest craving. "Boy, if those walls could talk."

"I know I'll always love that building," John commented, sliding an arm around my shoulders. He kissed my forehead. "That's where I met you."

There he went, turning me to mush again. I grinned at him, leaning into his chest. "The one time I'm glad I went to a party."

"Y'all sure you have everything?" Russell asked us. He'd been pretty quiet since he got there and I knew my leaving was probably kicking in for him.

"Yep. The house is empty and the moving trucks are full."

"We'll be in Brodence before we know it," John added. "And I can't wait until they unpack the bed or the couch because I'm collapsing on whichever one is down first."

"Save some room for me 'cause I'll be right behind you."

"Gotta christen the new house, huh?" Norelle asked, stuffing the last of her breadstick into her mouth. "You're gonna end up pregnant like me, the way y'all probably go at it. Horny asses."

"We were talking about *sleeping*, Norelle," I corrected, amused. "We're exhausted. I swear your mind stays in the gutter."

"Uh-huh."

"Babe, we'd better get going," John informed me, glancing at his watch. "We wanted to try to have everything unloaded before dark."

"Right. Okay."

He leaned in and kissed my cheek. "Take a minute with them," he murmured in my ear. "I'll be in the car."

I smiled at him gratefully as he stepped back. After waving to my friends, he got in the front seat of his Maxima.

When I looked at Dixie, she was already crying but trying to keep a smile on her face. Russell had his arm around Norelle, who looked emotional but at least wasn't crying. And Russell looked like someone had just stolen his PlayStation.

"We agreed we weren't gonna do this," I reminded them, pointing both fingers. "I thought we got all of the sad, emotional stuff out of the way already."

"Well, I can't help it," Dixie defended. "It's hard to be cheerful about you leaving."

"I honestly didn't expect it to hit me this hard," Russell admitted. "But it's all in good spirit. We'll get used to the idea soon enough."

"Make sure you call us when you get there," Norelle chimed in. "Lord, I'm sounding like a mama already."

That at least got us all laughing, to my relief. I didn't want to leave them on a sad note. Sure, my moving was a change and would take some getting used to, but it wasn't a bad thing. Our friendships weren't changing. I'd still be there for them and I knew they'd still be there for me.

"Y'all will need to come see us once we get settled," I told them as Dixie took hold of my arm. "I love our new house. Maybe y'all can even stay the weekend; it's not like I'm not used to you all crashing my spot. And Dixie, I'll be back in a couple of weeks to go dress shopping with you."

"I can't wait," she grinned.

Norelle grabbed my other arm. "And I'll be calling you to let you know about my doctor's visit on Monday. We're gonna find out what we're having then, too."

"Good. I wanna hear how our little snickerdoodle is progressing and if we're gonna have a mini Norelle or a mini Russell running around."

Russell stepped forward and kissed my forehead before wrapping his long arms around Dixie and Norelle's shoulders, and we all pulled into a group hug. "Look at us, making grown-up moves and shit."

"Speaking of that, Russell, we need to go to Toast and Butter when we leave here," Norelle informed him.

"What in the world does that have to do with what I said?"

"Nothing. I'm just hungry and want some pancakes."

"I'm actually a little jealous," I mused. "I wish we had time to go with y'all."

"Ahh-ha, that's what you get for moving."

"Shut up, Norelle."

"We'll all go when you come back to visit," Dixie suggested. "We'll sit at our favorite table and pig out."

"Sounds good." I smiled at her before looking at all of them, feeling something wash over me. I really was gonna miss them.

"You'd better get going, Lola," Russell ordered, glancing back at John in the car. "I'm sure y'all wanna beat the traffic and all that."

"Yeah. Plus we still have to finish getting everything moved in." I stepped back. "I'll let you know when we get there."

"You'd better."

Giving them all one more individual hug, I scurried to John's car and got in. We had already driven mine to our new house the previous weekend and parked it in the garage, and had been sharing John's since then. Good thing I hardly went anywhere.

"Ready, babe?" John asked, clamping a hand on my thigh.

I glanced at my onlooking friends before smiling at him. "Yep. Ready."

He leaned over to give me a lingering kiss before starting the engine. With one more wave to my friends, we pulled off, heading for Brodence and whatever was there waiting for us.

I hope you enjoyed this compilation of my Introvert series. What started off as an in-between project with *An Introvert's Christmas* stretched out into four fun stories, and I loved writing 'em. Lola was such a fun character to create, not to mention her silly friends.

And I hope you dug the bonus story, *Goodbye, Introvert.*

If I can ask a teeny favor of you, please consider leaving a review of this and any other story of mine you enjoy. Reviews are invaluable, especially to us indies. ☺

Oh, and as for all the socials, you can find me on Instagram and TikTok at @AuthorJessicaTerry, on Twitter at @ItsJessicaTerry. Facebook, too (facebook.com/ JessicaTerryBooks). You can also join my low-key email list at www.jessicaterry.com[1].

Also by Jessica Terry

Did you love *The Introvert Series Compilation*? Then you should read *All Because of Ava*[1] by Jessica Terry!

Ava and Harper's honeymoon phase came to a screeching halt as soon as she met Mario.

Ava battled with the guilt of fantasizing about one man while being married to another...even if the one she was married to increasingly felt like a stranger the more she learned about him.

Mario knew Ava was taken, but that didn't stop him from wanting her. And when he and Ava keep getting thrown

---

1. https://books2read.com/u/3LV7ZM

2. https://books2read.com/u/3LV7ZM

together, the sparks can't help but fly, despite their efforts to resist.

Pretty soon Ava, Mario, and Harper are in a very weird, very uncomfortable love triangle that is a ticking time bomb waiting to explode. And when it does, the damage may be irreparable.

Read more at https://www.jessicaterry.com/.

About the Author

Jessica Terry caught the writing bug at a young age and loves little more than holing up at home in Douglasville, GA, cranking out contemporary novels. And eating.

Another thing she loves is interacting with her readers. Sign up for her email list and keep up to date with new releases at www.jessicaterry.com.

Read more at https://www.jessicaterry.com/.

www.ingramcontent.com/pod-product-compliance
Lightning Source LLC
Chambersburg PA
CBHW032208170626
46808CB00006B/2388